THE HIDDEN GOVERNESS: A REGENCY ROMANCE

LADIES ON THEIR OWN: GOVERNESSES AND COMPANIONS

ROSE PEARSON

THE HIDDEN GOVERNESS

Ladies on their Own: Governesses and Companions

(Book 2)

By

Rose Pearson

© Copyright 2022 by Rose Pearson - All rights reserved.

In no way is it legal to reproduce, duplicate, or transmit any part of this document by either electronic means or in printed format. Recording of this publication is strictly prohibited and any storage of this document is not allowed unless with written permission from the publisher. All rights reserved.

Respective author owns all copyrights not held by the publisher.

THE HIDDEN GOVERNESS

PROLOGUE

"You *will* wed him."

Lady Albina Waterford lifted her chin and looked directly into her father's eyes.

"I shall not."

Her father's eyes narrowed.

"I will not tolerate such behavior, Albina. I have already spoken to you about Lord Kingston and explained to you the particulars as best I could."

Shaking her head firmly, Albina kept her gaze fixed on her father.

"What you have said, father, is that the gentleman I am engaged to was found in the most deplorable of situations and that I, somehow, am meant to ignore such a thing and continue on with our marriage!"

Her father threw up his hands.

"Why should you not? The *ton* does not know of it yet so there can be no scandal." Albina closed her eyes, wondering why her father could not see the difficulty in this particular situation. To encourage your daughter into wedlock was one thing, but to push her towards a gentleman who had been discovered in a less than honorable situation was quite another. That did not speak well of his character and Albina had always promised herself she would choose her husband wisely. "The situation with the house of disrepute is an unfortunate one, but that should not deter you, my dear girl." Her father's tone was gentler now as if he were trying to cajole her into doing as he wished. "But I can assure you that it will not continue."

"Except that is not something you can promise," she protested, quickly. "I have spoken to Lord Kingston myself on this matter and he was eager to inform me that such visits to places of disrepute would not continue once we were wed. Clearly, father, he is a gentleman who delights in frequenting such places. I am not inclined towards him in that regard, I am afraid."

"And so, you shall insist on ending the engagement?"

"I shall." Albina was undeterred. "There will be, of course, a few mutterings through society, but I can see no difficulty with that."

The Earl of Rutherford blinked slowly at her, in a somewhat owl-like fashion. He tipped his head, drew in a long breath, and then let it out very slowly indeed.

"No, you shall marry Lord Kingston. I have spoken with Lord Kingston, and I am convinced that he has every intention of behaving honorably."

Albina caught her breath. Her father had always promised that she would not be forced into matrimony with anyone, so why now was he insisting upon Lord Kingston?

"Father, I –"

"I am not inclined towards coming back to London for another Season. Besides which, if you do not wed Lord Kingston then the *ton* will talk, and there will be questions raised as to why you did *not* marry. That will, unfortunately, lead to a lack of interest in you." Leaning forward, his eyes pierced her heart. "They will speak of you, but they will not be eager for your company."

"I am sure that will pass," Albina returned. "I cannot marry Lord Kingston! I –"

"You can and you will." Lord Rutherford rose from his chair, indicating that the conversation was at an end. "Lord Kingston expects it, and I will be contented with him."

"But *I* shall not be!" Albina cried, refusing to remove herself from her father's study. "I am afraid I shall insist, father. I will not marry him."

Lord Rutherford came over towards her and Albina shrank back in her chair. Her breathing grew quicker at the sight of her father's narrowed eyes and lowered brows. He was furious with her.

"One way or the other, you will stand up beside him and make your promises, Albina." His voice was low, the words hissed out from between clenched teeth. "I have means by which to make certain that you do as you are told. Do you understand me?" Albina swallowed hard. The fire of anger that had swept through her only seconds ago was now being blown out, leaving her with nothing but smoke and ashes. "Now return to your bedchamber! You will dine alone this evening. I have no wish to see you again today. And when Lord Kingston proposes, Albina, you *will* accept. Now, go!"

There was nothing for her to do but stumble out of his study and back towards her room. Tears blurred her vision, her feet dragging as the realization of her future hit her. She would be wed to Lord Kingston who, on the outside, appeared just as every gentleman ought, but on the inside had a character so despicable that she would find not even the smallest modicum of contentment with him.

A gasping sob broke from her lips as she reached her bedchamber. Her hand slipped on the doorknob, and it took her three attempts to push it open. Hurrying inside, Albina sank down onto her bed and put her head in her hands.

Her future was nothing but darkness and shadow. Lord Kingston was not the honorable man she'd thought him. Albina recalled when she had first tried to speak to him about the night he had been found with a number of ladies in the house of disrepute. All he had spoken of was his relief that the *ton* would not be aware of it. The gentleman who had discovered him – in a state of intoxication, it seemed – had been a friend of Lord Rutherford's and thus, the matter had been kept quiet, although Albina was certain that a good deal of coin had changed hands. Lord Kingston had not apologized for being found in such company; he had not begged her to forgive him nor expressed any sort of sorrow about such goings on. Instead, he had thought to laugh, to press her hand and promise – albeit with a gleam in his eye – that once they were wed, he would not do such a thing again.

Albina did not believe him.

But what am I to do now?

Albina dropped her hands from her face and attempted to think clearly. Her thoughts were still swarming together, and she struggled to pull them apart into a calm, coherent order. Rising, she walked to her dressing table and sat down.

"If you are not to wed Lord Kingston, then what are you to do?"

Her reflection did not answer her, and Albina's shoulders dropped. There was no simple answer, no easy way for her to find a solution to her predicament. She had no doubt that her father *would* find a way to force her into wedlock if he chose to do so. One way or the other, he would have her standing at the front of the church. *And even if I do not make my vows, that will not matter.* She had seen it before. A young lady made the smallest of sounds, and it was taken for an assent. Would her father truly go as far as to force her to do that?

Her head dropped. Her father was not a kind man, and he had never really shown any sort of consideration for Albina, aside from promising her that she should have the opportunity to choose the gentleman she tied herself to for the rest of her days. Now, it seemed, he had decided to break that promise, simply so that he could have an easier life for himself. With no daughter to consider, he would have nothing but his estate, his wife, and his own pleasures to concern him.

An aching sob lodged itself in Albina's heart, sending pain throbbing through her chest. She dropped her head into her hands once more, tears streaming from her eyes and through her fingers.

Just what was she to do?

CHAPTER ONE

"What is it now?"

Patrick scowled as his butler walked into the room, a silver tray in hand.

"You have a letter, my Lord."

Sighing heavily, Patrick snatched it from the tray.

"Did I not say that I was not to be interrupted?"

The butler inclined his head.

"You did, my Lord, but you also stated that you wished to be brought any correspondence the moment it arrived. I am sorry if I mistook your direction."

Grimacing, Patrick did not answer. As much as he did not want to admit it, Patrick knew the butler spoke the truth. Breaking the seal on his letter, he pulled it open and quickly read the contents.

His mouth flattened.

"I am being sent a governess." The butler said nothing. "I did inform you that I wrote to Mrs. Patterson?"

His servant nodded.

"You did, my Lord."

"Well, it seems that she has found someone more than suitable and the lady will be joining us by the end of the week!" This, whilst a relief, did not take away from the fact that he still had a nephew to care for – a situation which he did not like in the least. "The child will no longer be able to run about this house as though he owns every single room within it." Folding up the letter, he set it back on the tray. "Have that put in my study."

Nodding, the butler turned.

"Of course."

"And make preparations for the governess," Patrick called after him. "Oh, and do send up Lord Newford whenever he arrives."

Whether or not the butler said anything, Patrick did not know. He did not care. He expected that his orders would be followed without question and without any fraction of hesitation. Sighing contentedly, Patrick leaned his head back and allowed his eyes to close – just as he had been doing before the butler had so rudely interrupted him. Having spent some time in London, Patrick had returned to his estate so that he might enjoy more *select* company and the first of his house parties was already at an end, which explained his great fatigue. He smiled to himself. It had been a most enjoyable few days and the next house party was already planned for the end of the following week! His staff would find the task arduous, he was sure, but that did not concern him. He had wealth and, if required, he would simply hire staff to replace those who complained.

And now the governess is coming.

That made his smile spread even further. The governess would take care of his nephew Henry, which would permit Patrick to have just as much freedom as he normally would.

This last house party had, unfortunately, had a few moments when he had been called away to deal with issues arising from the child. With no governess to speak of, and only two young maids to try to take care of him, Henry was proving himself to be a rambunctious young man who irritated Patrick terribly - both by his actions, and by the fact that his very existence reminded Patrick of all that he had lost. At only four years of age, Henry seemed to manage to slip away from the maids whenever he wished and had often been found roaming the halls of Patrick's great estate. *And the library.* Patrick's lip curled at the memory. He had been very close to stealing a kiss from one of the young ladies who had come to call for the house party and, had it not been for Henry throwing open the library door and stepping inside, Patrick was sure he would have succeeded.

"Not that I cared for the chit at all."

Scrubbing one hand down his face and letting his voice bounce around the room, Patrick sighed aloud and settled his head back again. He just needed a few moments of rest before Lord Newford came to call. Patrick had something he had recently purchased to show him – something that he knew would make Lord Newford more than a little envious, and that thought brought Patrick a lot of delight. To possess more than other gentlemen, to have a title greater than the majority of gentlemen – these things Patrick clung onto with both hands. For what good was wealth if it could not be held aloft, over the heads of other gentlemen, who might then, in turn, wish that they could be as he was?

"Lord Newford, my lord."

Patrick jerked in surprise, having been tugged out of his thoughts by the knock on the drawing-room door.

"Yes, of course."

Throwing himself out of his chair, he straightened his jacket and then grinned broadly at Lord Newford as he walked into the room.

Lord Newford was smaller in stature than Patrick, with narrowed, shifting green eyes which seemed to look everywhere at once. Patrick chuckled and walked towards him, shaking Lord Newford's hand firmly.

"Good afternoon, good afternoon!" he exclaimed, as Lord Newford only managed the smallest of smiles which disappeared the very next moment. "I am very glad that you were able to call today"

Lord Newford's eyes narrowed all the more, until only two small slits were seen.

"I am sure there is a reason for your interest in having me call, Lord Addenbrook."

Patrick grinned.

"Not at all! Would you care for some refreshments?" He gestured for the gentleman to sit down, and, after a moment of further scrutiny, Lord Newford did so. "Let me ring the bell."

Once he had done so, Patrick sat back down opposite Lord Newford with a sense of growing anticipation tightening his chest. This had all been thoroughly planned and Patrick was confident that his servants would not let him down.

"You had a most enjoyable house party, I trust?"

Patrick nodded.

"It was excellent," he confirmed, wondering if there was a hint of jealousy in Lord Newford's remark. "I should be glad to invite you to one of my other house parties which I have planned."

Lord Newford's eyebrows rose.

"You have another planned?"

"I have another *three* planned!" Patrick laughed. "I left London for the sole purpose of throwing such house parties so that I might be blessed with the company of those I choose."

Lord Newford blinked.

"I see."

The fact that Lord Newford had not expressed any sort of amazement that Patrick would do such a thing and, rather, appeared more surprised, irritated him.

"I have the wealth for such things, as you know, so why should I not have the very best of company?"

Lord Newford smiled tightly but did not say anything. Patrick's lips pulled flat, his brow furrowing. This was not what he had expected. He had thought that Lord Newford would admire him for such a thing, would think him quite the gentleman for having more than one house party in the Season but instead, Lord Newford simply sat there, saying very little.

The scratch at the door indicated the arrival of the tea tray and, much to Patrick's delight, the item that he knew Lord Newford would react to.

"Come in."

He watched the maid come in with the tea tray and then, stepping out for the second time, come back in with another tray which held a single item covered with a cloth.

Lord Newford's eyes flicked to it, but he did make any remark. Patrick smiled to himself, already expecting to garner much satisfaction from Lord Newford's reaction.

"Now, before we partake, I should like to show you something."

With one outstretched hand, he reached for the cloth covering the item, ready to pull it back. His eyes were fixed upon Lord Newford and, as he pulled the cloth back, he waited expectantly for the man to gasp or to let out some sort of exclamation – and he was not disappointed. Lord Newford's eyes flared wide, and he stared down at the item. He appeared utterly transfixed and Patrick leaned back in his chair, satisfied.

"You have a Turner."

"I do," Patrick replied, grinning. "I know that you are a great admirer of Joseph Turner's paintings and thus, I decided to purchase one."

Lord Newford's eyes flicked to Patrick and then back to the painting. His eyes were still wide, but he eventually sat back, his arms crossing over his chest as he dragged his gaze away from the painting.

"You decided to purchase the most expensive of all of his works thus far, I see."

"I did." Patrick shrugged, that same feeling of contentment running through him, curling up into a ball of satisfaction. "I thought it would be an excellent addition to my current collection."

Lord Newford closed his eyes briefly, then tried to smile. It was not a particularly strong smile, however, and quickly faded.

"Shall we have coffee? I do not want to be away from my estate for too long and, as you know, it takes me a little over an hour to reach you."

"Of course."

Patrick poured the coffee quickly then gestured to Lord Newford to take it. There was nothing Patrick liked more than showing his wealth and possessions to others. He did not care whether they thought little of him because of it – he had plenty of friends who were glad of his company *and* his wealth, without even allowing a single hint of jealousy into their friendship with him. Lord Newford, he knew, had been eager to own a painting by Turner and, now that Patrick had found himself in a position to purchase one, he'd had only one thought: to show the painting to Lord Newford. The man would, no doubt, be envious of Patrick's wealth and standing but that was just as Patrick liked it. He wanted to continually remind those near to him that, as a Marquess, he was far above them in terms of his title *and* his fortune and this was, he had found, one of the best ways to achieve such a thing.

"You asked me here to show me the Turner painting, then?"

Lord Newford's eyebrow lifted, and Patrick shrugged.

"I thought you would appreciate it."

"You thought that it would show you in the best light, no doubt," Lord Newford shot back, quickly. "I am to be reminded once more of your substantial wealth and that nothing is beyond your reach, is that not so?"

Patrick laughed, trying to throw the remark aside without being required to answer it – but at that moment, the door flew open and a small, dark-haired figure rushed into the room.

All of Patrick's smiles fled as the small boy charged forward, spinning in-between the chairs and screeching at the top of his voice.

"Henry!"

The boy did not respond. Patrick rose to his feet and used his most commanding voice.

"That is enough! Take yourself back to the nursery this instant!"

Instead of responding meekly and doing as Patrick had asked, Henry merely let out a shriek of laughter and attempted to run straight past Patrick.

Reaching out one hand, Patrick grabbed the boy's arm

and pulled him back... directly into the table and the tea tray set upon it. The tray was upended from the force of Henry's small frame slamming against it, and the coffee itself decided to make its way in a beautiful arc towards the Turner painting.

Silence fell.

All Patrick heard was the sound of his heavy breathing as his eyes fixed themselves to the now coffee-splattered painting.

And then, Lord Newford chuckled.

Every part of Patrick's frame tightened.

"I think I shall leave you to your painting, Lord Addenbrook."

Rising from his chair, Lord Newford reached forward and ruffled Henry's hair. The boy jumped in surprise, threw a quick look at Patrick, and then ran from the room.

Patrick could not miss the glee in Lord Newford's expression.

"Good afternoon, Lord Addenbrook. I do hope that you find the very best place for that particular picture to hang. I am sure it will take pride of place in your collection, as you have said. Goodbye."

There was not enough grace in Patrick's character to permit him to bid Lord Newford farewell. He was left utterly mortified with his painting now dripping wet with coffee and the carpet completely soaked. The small boy in his care was gone but had left a trail of destruction behind him.

Patrick's hands curled into fists as his mounting temper began to burn hot. *That little brat.* The child he did not want, the child he had been forced to take on, had ruined his afternoon – and his standing – in front of Lord Newford. Throwing open the door, Patrick stormed through his manor house, shouting for his butler, for the maid, for the footman, and in particular, demanding that the small boy who had caused so much trouble stayed out of his sight for the remainder of the day.

That governess could not come soon enough.

CHAPTER TWO

"Thank you for taking me in."

Albina's voice was trembling as she grasped the hands of her old governess.

"I truly did not know who to turn to."

"That is quite all right, my dear. Now, drink this cup of tea and we will soon have you rested."

Albina, hot and weary from her journey – some of which had required her to walk – sank down into an old, rickety wooden chair that felt more comfortable than anything she had ever sat on at home. Tears burned in her eyes, and she let them fall. This last fortnight had been the most tumultuous of her life and Albina had never felt so fatigued.

"I am very sorry to hear of your troubles." Mrs. Stanley sat down opposite her, her lined face gentle. "That sounds very trying."

"It has been," Albina agreed, softly. "I had nowhere else to go, no-one to turn to, save you."

A plan had quickly been formed whereby Albina had

left everything she owned behind and had made her way to the home of her old governess, who had, with Albina's pin money, purchased what would be needed for her new position as governess. However, given all that had been required to be purchased, Albina now had only a few meager coins left.

"And I am very glad to have been of help to you. I am sure we were brought together at the right time, given that my sister spoke to me of a Marquess seeking a governess at exactly the same time as your letter arrived."

The knot of tension that had been in Albina's stomach tightened still further.

"I am not sure I shall be very good as a governess."

"Yes, you shall." The confidence in Mrs. Stanley's voice did not bring Albina any further encouragement. "You were a good child and you learned quickly. I am certain that you will do the same in this situation too."

Albina managed a small smile and then took a sip of her tea.

"My mother will, I am certain, be searching for me."

"I can understand your sorrow in leaving home."

Swallowing the lump in her throat, Albina stared down dejectedly at her teacup.

"I had no other choice."

"Your father wished you to marry a gentleman you disliked?"

"More than disliked," Albina replied, heavily. "He was a gentleman inclined to his own pleasures who cared nothing for my heart. I believed him to be entirely honorable until a certain situation came to light."

Her old governess nodded.

"I quite understand. I was blessed to find a husband

much later in life, which was the only reason I was able to step back from my position as governess. But had I been at all uncertain of him, I would have remained as governess." Reaching across, she put one hand on Albina's knee. "You have my sympathies and my understanding."

Tears dripped from Albina's eyelashes despite her attempts to hold them back.

"Thank you."

"Come now, child, try not to cry. You are tired and things will look a little brighter in the morning."

Albina nodded, her whole body aching with weariness.

"Lord Addenbrook's estate is not far from here. If anything should go wrong, then you need only make your way back. You will always have a welcome here, Albina."

Pressing her lips together, Albina dried her eyes with her handkerchief, which she had only just pulled from her sleeve.

"Do you know how long you intend to be a governess for?" Mrs. Stanley's voice was gentle. "I understand that you wish to escape from a forced betrothal, but will you remain with Lord Addenbrook indefinitely?"

Albina's voice wobbled.

"I am not certain. I did not think about what else I would do once I became a governess, only that I had to escape from the situation which my father had placed me in, with all haste."

Mrs. Stanley nodded slowly, seeming to understand Albina's confusion.

"There is a lot to think of, and mayhap you are right to take this situation just as it stands, until you are certain what you wish to do next."

Another worry plagued Albina's mind.

"Might I ask what you know of Lord Addenbrook's character? He is a gentleman, I understand."

She bit her lip, worried that Lord Addenbrook might dislike her immediately and have her role stripped from her by the end of her first day at his estate.

"He is the Marquess of Addenbrook so yes, he is certainly a gentleman!" Mrs. Stanley laughed, as Albina nodded. "I will be truthful with you, however. He is not the best of characters, from what I understand. Unfortunately, he has a great deal of wealth and is eager that everyone nearby knows just how fortunate he is." Her smile faded and Albina's spirits dropped. "He will not be cruel to you, however. I am sure that he will take very little notice of you, in fact! Which, under the circumstances, is probably best."

"Indeed." Albina took another sip of her tea, her hands clasped around the chipped cup. It was a far cry from her previous situation, but Albina had told herself from the beginning that she could not expect to live in the way she had always been accustomed to. If she was to escape from Lord Kingston and her father's demands, then she would have no other choice but to accept many changes – which included changing her delicate china cups for chipped ones. "And the child's name?"

Mrs. Stanley's brow furrowed, her eyes shifting across the room.

"That would be Henry if I remember correctly. My sister read the letter to me, and I am certain that is the name she said. He is only a few years of age – four, I think – and is Lord Addenbrook's nephew."

"And how did he come to live with him?"

"That, I do not know," Mrs. Stanley confirmed. "I do not think he clarified that, but he said that the presence of a governess was required immediately."

Albina's lips twisted.

"I do hope I can fulfill his requirements."

"He requires someone to look after the child so that he does not have to spare a maid or two to do it," her old governess stated firmly. "The maids and the housekeeper, and perhaps even the butler, will be exasperated enough already. Your arrival will be most welcome."

Nodding, Albina tried to smile despite the mounting nervousness growing like a weed within her.

"And Lord Addenbrook will not attempt to converse with me or the like?"

"No, he will not. In most houses, the master is, as you know yourself, caught up with his own affairs and more than eager to allow the care of his charges to be given to someone capable. *You* are capable, Albina."

"I must hope so." Hesitating, Albina looked back steadily at her old governess before she asked her next question. "You were always very kind to me, Mrs. Stanley. To your mind, does such kindness encourage a child to obey their governess?"

Mrs. Stanley's lined face split with a smile.

"My dear girl, of course it does," she answered, softly. "The child you will care for will need a good deal of kindness and consideration. They must come to trust you, to know that you mean nothing but good for them. Do not expect immediate obedience but give yourself and the child enough time to get to know one another. And write to me, if you need a little advice. You know I will be glad to give it."

Albina closed her eyes and took in a deep breath, thinking carefully about everything that Mrs. Stanley had just told her. Were she to be honest with the lady and with herself, Albina would admit that she was terrified. Terrified that she would ruin everything by her lack of experience, that her charge would soon realize that she was *not* a real governess and that she would be removed from her position before a sennight was through.

"You will be the very best governess, my dear girl." As if she had been able to tell what Albina was thinking, Mrs. Stanley reached over and took Albina's hand in her own. "I have every faith in you."

Her heart twisted but Albina nodded, managing a small smile.

"Thank you, Mrs. Stanley. Thank you for everything."

~

DROP YOUR HEAD. *You must remember to be deferential.*

It took an effort and a lot of internal reminders for Albina to finally lower her head a fraction. Had she been here as Lady Albina, then she would have walked into Lord Addenbrook's home and greeted him as any other lady of the *ton* might. But she was now no longer in her position as the daughter of an Earl and had to behave as such.

Lowering her eyes, Albina balled one hand into a fist but kept both hands by her side. Her head down, she waited for the butler to speak to Lord Addenbrook before she was allowed to enter.

The large oak door to his study was finally pulled back for her and Albina drew in a long breath before stepping forward.

"And this is the governess, then?"

"Miss Ann Trean, Lord Addenbrook."

With some trepidation, Albina walked into the room, keeping her gaze fixed on the floor. The room was a little dim and smelt of mahogany. This was an expensive gentleman's room indeed! Albina allowed herself a small glance about the room but did not look at her employer. It was beautifully furnished. There were little touches here and there, all evidence of the wealth that Lord Addenbrook possessed.

"Are you going to search every nook and cranny of this room, or might you actually have any willingness to look at me?"

Albina winced inwardly at the sharp tone of Lord Addenbrook's voice and lifted her gaze to his for just a fraction of a second before dropping her eyes again. Lord Addenbrook was tall, broad-shouldered, and with a square jaw that was currently tightened in frustration. His eyes were dark and his hair a mid-brown, swept back from his forehead. A slight frown pulled at his brow and his arms were crossed over his chest.

"You look much too young to be a governess." His voice was low. "I do hope you will be able to keep the child in line."

Clearly, Albina had displeased him by both her lack of attention and her appearance.

"Forgive me, Lord Addenbrook." Her voice was thin, and Albina swallowed the knot which had formed in her throat. "I will be able to fulfill my duties, of course. In becoming distracted as I came in, I –"

I do not need to make up some excuse. I am just the child's companion, nothing more.

Lord Addenbrook had not moved from his chair and even as she spoke, Albina could tell that he was disinterested in what she was saying. He wasn't even looking at her any longer. Instead, his gaze was drifting from one corner of the room to the other and he remained quite silent for some minutes, even after Albina had finished speaking.

The butler cleared his throat.

Lord Addenbrook's eyes lifted back to Albina.

"Well?"

He threw up his hands as if she ought to know precisely what it was that he meant by it. Flustered, Albina turned to the butler, stammering an apology for not knowing what it was she was meant to do.

"I shall take you to Henry now." The butler's eyes turned to the door and Albina hurried towards it, turning her back on Lord Addenbrook. She was hot with embarrassment but, as she glanced over her shoulder and saw him pouring a measure of brandy into a glass, she became aware of a nudge of anger in her heart. It was not as though Lord Addenbrook had made any attempt to welcome her into the house, nor had given her any explanation about her role and expected duties. He had not even informed her of the boy's name or asked the butler to take her up to him! Albina's lips twisted. The very least Lord Addenbrook could have done would have been to introduce her to the child himself. Had not Mrs. Stanley said that the child was his nephew? Did he not care about him one whit?

"You will soon learn, Miss Trean, that the master does not like to be disturbed."

Albina swallowed her anger and glanced up at the butler.

"I understand."

"That will require you to keep the young man far from him at all times."

Biting her lip for a moment, Albina found her courage and asked a question that she feared would be a little too bold.

"Does Lord Addenbrook not wish to see his nephew at any time? Does he not have any interest in the child?"

The butler's head twisted towards her, and Albina's

stomach tightened, afraid that she had already made some sort of misstep.

"As I have said, you will soon learn about the master of this house, Miss Trean. He is not inclined to have any interest in the child, no. You should not expect it. He will not send for the boy, will not ask for any particular reports or the like."

Albina nodded, but silently considered that Lord Addenbrook appeared, thus far, to be the most dislikeable of gentlemen. Had she been in her proper situation, then she would have, most likely, done all she could to avoid him. *An arrogant fellow,* she thought to herself. *One who likes to think only of himself and his own interests.* Her lips pursed as she followed the butler up the staircase. The manor house was grand indeed, but Albina was not overawed by it, given that her father's estate and manor house was just as grand. This was all familiar to her and she knew the many comforts a house like this could bring.

Which was why it then came as something of a shock when she was shown into her small bedchamber. Albina bit back a protest as the butler ushered her in, reluctance growing with every step she took. The bare boards on the floor wrapped a draft around her ankles and the small window was murky with dirt.

"The maids were not given adequate time to clean, but the bed is prepared and the wardrobe ready. If you wish to have it a little tidier then I shall send up the necessary things."

The thought of having to clean her windows and sweep the dusty floor made Albina wince. The butler caught her expression and Albina, recalling immediately that she was pretending to be a governess well used to such a situation, quickly smiled.

"Thank you. I would be glad if you could do so."

"Good." The butler turned and walked smartly out of the room. "We have not made particular introductions as yet, of course." As Albina followed him into the hallway, he turned and gave her a short bow. "I am Mr. Carlisle. The housekeeper is Mrs. Meads."

"I am pleased to meet you."

Albina was not quite certain what a governess ought to say to a butler but this, much to her relief, seemed to suffice for the butler nodded and then gestured to the room opposite.

"This would be the schoolroom. You may peruse it at your leisure but, for the moment, I will take you to Master Henry."

Albina's swirling nervousness suddenly grew into a crescendo as the butler led her just a few steps along the hallway, knocking lightly on the door and then gesturing for her to step inside.

Her breath quickened, but she forced a smile to her lips and, pushing the door open, walked inside.

The room was dimly lit. One figure was bending over the small child as he lay in bed whilst another – a maid, Albina assumed, was tugging the drapes tightly closed.

"Who are you?"

The small voice came winding its way towards her and chased some of Albina's nervousness away. Keeping her smile on her face, she walked a little further into the room, just as the maids both melted away into the corner.

It was time to meet her charge.

"Good evening, Henry. I am your new governess."

The small boy blinked back at her. His dark hair was swept to one side of his forehead, his big, brown eyes staring up at her. All in all, he looked rather angelic.

"I don't need a governess."

At the very next moment, the covers of the bed were thrown back, and Henry kicked at them hard, letting out a loud, petulant scream. The maids rushed towards him, and Albina stumbled back, her heart hammering furiously with the shock of it.

The butler stepped in at once, his eyes wide.

"Do be quiet!" he demanded, although the child ignored him completely. "Lord Addenbrook insists that you are silent!"

It was not until Albina's back touched the wall that she realized she had been backing away. She had no thought of what to do, no knowledge of what would be best to help the child – but now the butler and one of the maids were both looking at her expectantly and Albina's stomach rolled.

What am I going to do?

To them, she was a governess with previous experience of children, and yet, as she stood in the room watching Henry flail about, Albina struggled against self-doubt. If she could not calm Henry, if she could do nothing other than stand back here by the wall, then her ruse might soon be discovered, she would lose her position and might have no other choice but to return home – and to Lord Kingston.

'The child you will care for will need a good deal of kindness and consideration.'

Mrs. Stanley's words flew into Albina's thoughts, and she caught her breath. The butler and the maids were all practically shouting at the child and his response was clearly one of discontent. But if she were to try the opposite, just as Mrs. Stanley had told her, then was there a chance that Henry would react entirely differently?

Taking in a deep, steadying breath and trying to grasp hold of her fears, Albina stepped away from the wall and towards Henry. The boy was still yelling and kicking away the sheets that the maid was attempting to pull over him. With a confidence she did not really feel, Albina stayed the maid's hand, then sat down on the edge of the bed.

"Henry."

Her voice was quiet and calm and the child, whilst still shouting all manner of things, eventually glanced at her, his yells becoming a little more infrequent. Albina did not know what else to say but instead simply held out her arms to the small boy.

Henry looked up at her, then looked at her arms and the space she had created there. Albina's heart was pounding furiously and, whilst the room was silent, there was a great deal of tension still buzzing furiously around it. *Please, Henry,* she prayed silently, fully aware that the butler and the maid would relate everything she had done to the rest of the household staff.

And then, at the very next moment, Henry pushed himself up onto his knees and practically flung himself into Albina's arms. She caught him easily and held him close, her breathing quick and her eyes closing with relief.

"My goodness, I never would have thought of that."

As Albina looked up at them, she saw the two maids exchanging glances whilst the butler himself shook his head.

"We shall leave you to put the child to bed, then," he told her, making his way to the door, and gesturing for the maids to leave the room. "Let us hope, Miss Trean, that your success with the boy continues."

Albina said nothing. As she held Henry close to her, there came a sensation flooding her that she had never experienced before. It seemed to calm both herself and the boy for, after a few minutes, his head grew a little heavier on her shoulder and his breathing deepened.

She closed her eyes in relief. Without Mrs. Stanley's advice, she would never have been able to step forward with such boldness. This was clearly what Henry needed – some love and kindness rather than anger and irritation.

Perhaps she could do this after all.

CHAPTER THREE

"I still think she looks much too young for a governess."

Patrick's eyes narrowed as he watched Miss Trean and Henry walk across the grass in front of the manor house. They had their backs to him, given that they were just setting out on their daily excursion, but from the way that Henry was looking up at the lady, Patrick could tell that he was happy.

That makes one of us, at least.

"Did you say something?"

Clearing his throat, Patrick turned sharply away from the window.

"It was nothing of importance, merely a personal grumbling about my nephew." He tried to smile but it did not fully reach his lips. "It is very difficult when one's life is interrupted by a matter that simply cannot be resolved in any other way."

His friend, Lord Hogarth, nodded sagely as though to suggest that he too had some experience of what Patrick was expressing.

"Indeed. Although at least with the boy, you can send him to Eton when he is seven years of age. That is not too long from now, is it?"

Patrick rolled his eyes.

"He has only just turned four and whilst that may not appear to be a great length of time, it seems to stretch out to an eternity before I can remove him from this house!"

"And are you required to keep him?"

Nodding, Patrick reached for his brandy.

"You know that I am. There is no other alternative." He certainly had no intention of discussing the matter further at this juncture for, if he did, Patrick feared he would soon find himself in a state of melancholy and thus quickly changed the subject. "Now, you are to join me for the next house party, I hope?"

Lord Hogarth grinned.

"Of course! There is nothing that would prevent me from being here. I assume that you have invited the very best of the *ton* to join us?"

"I have." Quickly, Patrick reeled off a list of those he had invited and smiled to himself at the way Lord Hogarth's eyes widened. "There is also Lady Havisham and her companion, a Miss Fullerton –"

"Who, I presume, is not to be preyed upon given that she is the companion of Lady Havisham."

Patrick smiled wryly.

"It is exactly as you have stated it. However, the last are Lady Foster and her two elegant daughters."

"Both of whom are looking for a husband this Season, or so I have been told."

Lord Hogarth lifted one eyebrow, but Patrick only laughed.

"They will have to continue to look, for I shall be very

disappointing indeed," he told his friend, firmly. "I am afraid that I could not be prevailed upon to take on a wife. It would alter my entire situation and it is not something that I have any wish to even *think* of at present."

Lord Hogarth chuckled.

"Nor I. Although I shall be glad of the company of two such fine young ladies, as well as the others you have mentioned."

"Indeed, as shall I be." Patrick grinned at his friend. "I have heard that Lady Winthrop is also a little... lonely at present, given that her husband has been on the continent for some seven months now!"

"I shall keep that in mind." Lord Hogarth gestured to the paintings which were hung above the library fireplace. "And did you manage to have the Turner restored?"

Patrick grimaced.

"It will never hold the same value again." His thoughts grew dark as he recalled just how Henry had humiliated him in front of Lord Newford, albeit unintentionally. "Lord Newford's opinion of me must be significantly altered."

"If I am to be truthful, then I should inform you that Lord Newford has told many people about what occurred." Lord Hogarth's eyes narrowed as he looked back at Patrick steadily. "He does seem to be enjoying your humiliation."

Grimacing, Patrick rubbed at the spot between his eyebrows, trying to rid himself of some of the tension there.

"I suppose that is to be expected."

"Oh?"

"I only purchased the Turner to make sure that he saw it," Patrick stated, having no need to explain further given the friendship between the two men. "But given that he was also present during the incident with the coffee, I have never doubted that he would spread such news as best he could."

"I believe it has even reached London."

That stung Patrick's pride even more and he winced.

"Goodness. Then I shall have to do something extraordinary very soon if I am to maintain my reputation."

"And what might that be?"

Patrick sighed and flung out both arms, having already set his brandy down.

"I cannot say as yet but have no doubt, I will find something very soon."

˷

WHY HE WAS out in the gardens, Patrick was not really sure. After his conversation with Lord Hogarth, he had found himself a little restless and thus had decided to take a walk through the grounds. It was not something he did often and yet, as he walked across the grass with long, steady strides, Patrick had to admit to himself that there was something pleasant about it. The air was warm, the sky still a brilliant blue despite the lateness of the afternoon. A small smile crossed his lips as he continued to walk, thinking silently to himself that he ought to be taking full advantage of his estate at this time of year. Why, he could organize carriages so that when his guests arrived, they would be taken around the grounds and made fully aware of just how grand and expansive they were. That would, surely, encourage his guests to think well of him and to remind them of his standing as Marquess of Addenbrook, if they did not think highly enough of him already. His smile grew as the idea formed in his mind, to the point that he almost missed the young lady and the small boy playing in the grass beside the pond.

Patrick stopped and turned to face them, his hands clasped behind his back and his chest heaving with the exertion of walking so quickly. He hadn't been trying to find Miss Trean and Henry of course, but it could do no harm to simply allow himself to watch them for a few moments.

She appears to be much too young for a governess.

His lips curved as he watched Henry laugh, then throw a stone into the water which splashed lightly, near Miss Trean. In turn, she shrieked and then stepped back, her hands held up and away from the pond. For a moment, a memory surfaced in his mind, of himself as a child, Henry's father beside him, as they both threw stones into a pond. Sadness rose too, and he pushed it aside – Henry's presence reminded him of his loss, of his failure, all too much. But he stood there, still watching.

"Perhaps with her here, I will not feel Henry's presence in the house as much," Patrick muttered to himself, his hands squeezing tightly together as he watched them. He did not know how to deal with such a young boy. To his mind, Henry did nothing but either scream or cry and Patrick had no knowledge of what he ought to do in such a situation. However, with Miss Trean, it now seemed that Henry was far more settled and that must be a relief to them all.

"Henry, stop!"

Miss Trean's laughter rang out across the pond and Patrick found himself smiling. Realizing what he was doing, he forced the expression away from his face and turned on his heel, just as a twig snapped under his feet.

Miss Trean and Henry both turned to look towards him as one, leaving him with no other choice but to make his presence known. He watched the smile shatter from her face as he walked closer, noticed how Henry stepped closer to her, hiding his face in her skirts.

"Good afternoon, Miss Trean. I thought to take the air and came across you both."

Miss Trean bobbed a quick curtsey although her eyes looked directly into his thereafter, surprising him a little.

"Indeed, Lord Addenbrook. We try to come out for a short walk before dinner as I believe it is beneficial for Henry to do so."

"I see."

Patrick allowed his gaze to rove over Miss Trean as she looked down to where Henry stood, her hand ruffling his hair gently. Miss Trean was certainly young, with fair hair pulled back into a delicate chignon and blue eyes which seemed to pierce into his very soul whenever she looked at him. She was, Patrick had to admit, a rather handsome young lady, albeit a governess.

You know not to play with such creatures. Patrick cleared his throat and pulled his eyes away. He was not inclined towards flirting with any young lady who was not of the *ton*. Whilst Patrick enjoyed such flirtations, there was still the matter of conscience and to so treat a young lady who could not either defend herself or respond perhaps in the manner she wished would be most unfair. Besides which, Miss Trean was his nephew's governess and, given how well that appeared to be going, Patrick did not want to injure that in any way.

"I should take Henry back inside so that he is ready for dinner."

Miss Trean's eyes were sharp as Patrick looked back at her and he was surprised to see the flash of color in her cheeks. There was not any sense of delight nor delighted embarrassment in her face, however. Rather, there appeared to be only anger that he would look at her in such a way.

Patrick could not understand it. Had not most companions and governesses been overlooked by society? Surely, then, she would be glad of his momentary interest in her?

"Do excuse us, my Lord."

Without another word, Miss Trean turned her back on him and, with Henry's small hand clasped tightly in her own, began to walk smartly up the gentle slope back towards the house.

"Wait a moment!"

Patrick's mouth closed tight as Miss Trean turned to look back at him, one eyebrow lifting gently as though she were daring him to say something more. Patrick was a little nonplussed, not quite certain *why* he had asked her to stop and certainly without any idea of what it was he wished to say.

"I – I will walk with you."

It was a ridiculous thing to state, given that she was the governess and he the master of the house, but it was the only thing that he could think to come up with. If any of his servants saw him walking with her, they would wonder what he was doing walking with his nephew and his governess, since they were all very well aware that he had demanded that his nephew be kept away from him since the very moment he had arrived.

"But of course."

There was no smile on Miss Trean's face and certainly no eagerness in her voice. She sounded dull and a little frustrated, as though irritated that he now wished to walk with them. Patrick, bemused as to why he had said such a thing, had no other choice but to fall into step with her, all too aware that Henry had not said a single word since he had approached. In fact, the child was now clinging to Miss Trean's hand while continuing to hide his face in her skirts.

Patrick grimaced.

"He should not be clinging to you in such a fashion."

Miss Trean shot him a hard look.

"I believe that *I* am the governess, Lord Addenbrook."

Such temerity astonished him, and Patrick was robbed of speech for a few moments whilst Miss Trean simply continued to walk on, entirely unabashed.

"All the same, Miss Trean, I do believe that I might have some suggestions which could be of use to you."

Miss Trean did not even look at him this time.

"That may be a consideration of yours, my Lord, but it does not mean that I shall have the time to either listen or implement them." Her voice was calm and steady, and yet the way she spoke stole the very breath from his body. No servant, no hired help, had *ever* spoken to him in such a fashion and yet Miss Trean appeared to think nothing of it. Patrick did not know what to say nor how to respond. There was only the veil of astonishment hiding his other emotions from him as he swallowed against the tightness in his throat, trying his best to find a way to answer her. "After all, Lord Addenbrook, before I arrived, I believe that you had many opportunities to attempt your... suggestions on how best to deal with a child such as Henry, did you not?" Her gaze swung towards his, one eyebrow lifting gently. "Did you have much success?"

I did not want to even see the child.

Patrick's breathing grew quicker as he fought to find a response.

"I did not have an opportunity." It was a lie and, from the way that Miss Trean's lip curled, Patrick could tell precisely what she thought of his response. "I am sure that

Henry need not be such a dependent, stubborn child. You are his governess, Miss Trean. It is up to you to make certain that he does not remain so."

The way his voice rose sent Miss Trean's eyebrows higher up towards her hairline and Patrick allowed himself a small smile of satisfaction. He had managed to turn the conversation around.

"I hardly think that a four-year-old child needs to be told to stand on his own two feet, Lord Addenbrook, particularly when he has been sent into a new situation and told that his uncle does not want to see hide nor hair of him." The caustic tone burned through Patrick's skin and seared his heart with guilt. A guilt which he had never felt before, nor wanted to feel. "The boy needs nothing but love, compassion, and understanding and that is what I am offering him at present."

They had made their way to the door of the house and, with a broad, bright smile which told Patrick just how relieved she was to escape him, Miss Trean bid him farewell and then ushered Henry inside.

When Patrick walked into the house, he could hear Henry's giggles echoing down the staircase towards him. In the few seconds, it had taken for the child to be away from Patrick and again only with Miss Trean, he had changed from a quiet, clingy child into one who laughed with abandon.

I made it quite clear that I wanted nothing to do with the child.

Patrick dropped his head and ran one hand over his eyes. Why did he feel such a pinch of guilt now? He ought to be angry – furious, even – that Miss Trean had said such things to him and spoken with such forthrightness when she ought, instead, to have said very little and lowered her head, given her position.

He waited for that anger to surface, for the fire to begin to grow, but nothing came. Instead, the stab of shame that had pricked his heart seemed to grow in intensity. His shoulders rounded and he closed his eyes tight shut, willing the sensation to fade away.

But instead, it remained precisely where it was, choosing to make a permanent home in the depths of his heart and refusing to leave, no matter how much he begged it.

CHAPTER FOUR

"You should not have spoken to the Marquess that way." Albina looked back at her reflection in the small mirror which hung on the wall and frowned, her sea-blue eyes hard. "He will not think well of you for speaking in such a blunt manner."

Sighing, she put down her brush and attempted to smooth her hair back into a chignon. It had taken a bit of practice – a good deal of practice, in fact – but she now managed to do it without too much difficulty. Another long breath escaped her as she gazed at her reflection. She was nothing like her former self now.

The dreary grey day dress hung a little limply on her frame. There was no lace nor decoration on it now, for such a thing would be improper for a governess. There were no pearls around her throat, no diamonds glistening near her ears. Her hair was simple and unadorned.

The only beauty I have now is my eyes. Albina's shoulders sagged. *And even they look dull.* If she were honest with herself, if she dared to speak it aloud just to herself, Albina would admit that she missed her home. She missed the comforts which had been a part of her life since the day she was born. She missed her mother desperately, praying that the simple note Albina had left on her bed had been discovered, read, and kept safe by her mother. Tears pricked the corners of Albina's eyes as she remembered penning that note. It had told her mother the truth and had sworn to her that she would return home if there came any trouble or difficulty. If she closed her eyes, Albina could see her mother in her mind's eye, imagining her reading the note and then closing her eyes as tears ran down her cheeks. No doubt her father, however, would be quite the opposite. Already frustrated with her impertinence and stubbornness, he would have reacted with nothing short of anger. If she ever had cause to return home, Albina was uncertain as to the kind of welcome she would receive.

"I cannot leave now," she told herself, turning away from the mirror and smoothing her hands down her dress, making certain that she was prepared for the day. "Henry needs me."

A small smile chased away her melancholy. Despite all that she had been forced to endure thus far, despite the difficulties that had plagued her, the fears that burned in her mind, and the struggles that had bound her heart, Albina had found Henry to be a delightful young boy who simply needed her affection and her company. It had been just as Mrs. Stanley had said and for that, Albina was more than grateful.

These last few days, Albina had spent almost every waking moment with Henry. The child practically clung to her each and every morning, as if he had spent the night afraid that she would not be there come the morning. For a four-year-old, he was rather talkative - although as yet, he had not said a single word about either his mother or father and Albina had chosen not to ask. She had not even entered the schoolroom with Henry as yet, but had spent her time with him in the nursery or being out of doors in the garden – and Henry had blossomed. The screaming and kicking she had witnessed on her first evening had not repeated itself, and Henry had only asked to be held close each night before he went to sleep. Other times, he took her hand or found other ways to stay close to her, and Albina's heart could not help but soften towards him. Having had no experience of small children, it had not taken her long to realize that all Henry required of her was to listen, to laugh, to sing, and to smile – and whenever he smiled back at her, a little bit of her heart was stolen away.

Which was why it confused her all the more that Lord Addenbrook had not shown the smallest flicker of interest in his own flesh and blood.

A small scuffling sound made Albina's heart slam hard against her chest and she caught her breath. Turning around sharply, she looked out across the room but saw nothing. Her hand pressed against her heart, willing it to settle. She did not want to think of rats but, most likely, that was the reason for such a noise.

Drawing in a deep breath, Albina set her shoulders and walked to the door, trying to ignore the fact that tonight, she would be trying to sleep in her bed whilst rats scurried about the floor. It was not the first time she had heard such a noise, but it still startled her every time she heard it. Pulling open the door, Albina began to make her way to the schoolroom. Today, they would be starting their letters and she had a few things to prepare. Given that she had never taught a child their letters before, Albina was trying desperately to recall what Mrs. Stanley had taught her and *how* she had taught her so that she might then use the very same with Henry.

"Ah, Miss Trean."

A footman hurried towards her, a little out of breath from climbing so many stairs. "The master wishes to speak to you."

Albina frowned.

"I beg your pardon?"

"Lord Addenbrook requires your company. Now."

She blinked, then gestured to the schoolroom.

"I have to prepare for Henry's lessons."

The footman's eyes flared wide, and Albina immediately realized that she had made a mistake. A governess did not question the master in any way and did as they were requested without hesitation, just as any hired help would do. *But I do not like being pulled away from my task, given that my responsibility is first to Henry.* A knot of fear tied itself in her stomach as she looked longingly towards the schoolroom door. She had never taught letters before and needed this time to make certain that she was quite ready for Henry.

But it seemed that Lord Addenbrook was to steal that from her.

"Might I ask where Lord Addenbrook is at present?"

The footman, who had been gawping at her as if she were the most ridiculous creature he had ever seen, closed his eyes for a moment, opened them, and then pointed back down the stairs.

"He is in his study." His head swiveled back towards her. "And he is waiting."

Albina nodded and followed the footman without any further hesitation. A little embarrassed, she was all too aware that what she had said would soon become well known to the rest of the staff, for the footman would be eager to share what he had heard. Telling herself that such a thing did not matter – for a governess did not dine with the servants – Albina drew herself up to her full height and made her way directly towards the study.

Lifting one hand to rap on the door, Albina hesitated, biting her lip gently. She had no knowledge of what it was that Lord Addenbrook wanted, but she feared now that it was due to her forthright manner yesterday afternoon. Her mouth went dry as she imagined him telling her that she was now dismissed from her role. She would have to return to Mrs. Stanley and, perhaps, even to her family. *And what would become of Henry?*

The door opened, startling her.

"Do come in, Miss Trean." Lord Addenbrook arched one eyebrow. "I did hear your footsteps coming along the hallway and then noticed that they stopped just outside my door. But you did not knock."

Her face grew warm as she stepped inside, biting back the response that she wanted to shoot at him. *You cannot risk his ire.* Keeping her back straight, Albina clasped her hands in front of her, lifted her chin gently, and stood a little back from his desk. Lord Addenbrook walked past her, and she caught a gentle scent of spice, sending a strange, twisting sensation into her core. A little confused at such a reaction, Albina dropped her head, giving herself the appearance of a demure and decorous governess.

"Now, Miss Trean. I have something to ask you."

"Yes, my Lord."

Keeping her head low and attempting to speak quietly, Albina silently prayed that he would not fling her from the house.

"I must ask you what Henry has said of his home here."

Her eyes shot to his.

"I beg your pardon?"

Lord Addenbrook smiled, and Albina dropped her gaze back to the floor.

"I mean to ask you what he has said of his time here. Has he mentioned to you why he is now residing with me?"

Albina shook her head.

"No, he has not. He has mentioned that his room is a little smaller than the one he had before and that he is sometimes cold, but that is all."

Darting a glance at Lord Addenbrook, she caught the dark frown which quickly melted away when he caught her watching him.

"That is not what I meant, Miss Trean."

She waited for him to explain, but he did not. Instead, he just watched her, his hazel eyes glinting with flickers of steel.

"Rather than sitting silently, might you be willing to explain to me what you meant?" she exclaimed, once more allowing her frustration to rise up within her as she struggled to hold it back. "I do not like to play guessing games when it comes to something as important as your nephew!"

"And that, Miss Trean, is where the difference is." Deciding that it was not worth her responding with any further questions, Albina retreated into silence, inwardly scolding herself for not being able to restrain her fiery temper. "You have come to care for my nephew already, even though you have been here less than a sennight."

"That is true."

"And he has not told you anything about why he has come here."

"For the second time, no, he has not."

The sharpness in her tone could not be hidden, but

Albina was exasperated. Lord Addenbrook appeared to be intent on only asking questions but choosing not to answer them.

"I see." He tilted his head and his brown hair slipped over to one side of his head. "You are a most unusual governess, Miss Trean."

Her chin lifted.

"If you mean that I am a little bolder than most then I shall accept that."

The fear that he would remove her from her position faded away as she looked back steadily into his face. There was not anger there, but instead a flickering interest which glinted in his eyes. He tapped one finger repeatedly on the desk in front of him as he surveyed her

"My butler tells me that Henry has taken to you very well indeed and for that, I am glad." Clearing his throat, he rose from the desk and then came around beside her. "Please, sit down Miss Trean."

A little surprised, Albina blinked rapidly, then half turned to see him gesturing to two seats opposite each other. Her heart quickened. She had never been alone with a gentleman in such a way before and her instincts told her that all was not well. Ever since she had been a young girl, it had been made quite clear that she was never to sit down with a gentleman, to converse with a gentleman, or to walk out alone with a gentleman for the sake of propriety. And now Lord Addenbrook was asking her to do that very thing.

But I am not here as Lady Albina. I am here as Miss Trean, the governess.

She took in a breath and turned, sitting down as he had asked her, but the nervous anxiety which was rattling in her chest did not fade. As Lord Addenbrook sat down opposite, a shiver ran straight down her back at the intensity of his gaze. It lingered on her face and Albina had to fold her hands in her lap so that she would not push herself out of the chair and leave the room.

"You laid something of an accusation at my feet yesterday, Miss Trean."

Another shiver ran across her skin.

"An accusation?" Her voice was not light but rather a little tremulous. "I do not think –"

"You have made it quite plain that I am not as you think I ought to be with my nephew. No doubt my servants have informed you that I told them all to keep Henry away from me as best they could." When she did not respond, his jaw tightened, and he looked away. "I will not pretend that I did not do such a thing, Miss Trean. The truth is, I do not want Henry here, but I have not been given any other choice. He is now under my care, and I must endure his presence here until he is ready to go to Eton."

Albina's stomach turned over on itself, her fear that he might attempt to take advantage of her quickly fading. Her shoulders dropped as tension ran straight out of her fingers and onto the floor and the worry which had lined her features was now quickly replaced with a frown. Lord Addenbrook continued speaking, seemingly oblivious to her reactions.

"You think this very poor of me. I can see it in your features." Opening her mouth to say that yes, she *did* think this to be poor of him, given that Henry now appeared to have no mother or father of his own, Albina was then forced to snap her mouth shut when Lord Addenbrook continued regardless. "I have no time for children, Miss Trean. That is the very reason that you were hired. I do not wish to be interrupted by him, I do not want to be disturbed by his unruly behavior and I certainly do not want to see him when he is making the most appalling noise. That child is disorderly and must be given a firm hand."

"I shall disagree with you there, Lord Addenbrook." Despite telling herself inwardly that she needed to behave with submissiveness and appear nothing but humble before Lord Addenbrook, Albina could not help but speak. It was in the defense of Henry, after all, and she would not permit Lord Addenbrook to be harsh towards a little boy who needed nothing more than a kind word from him to behave in a much more appropriate fashion. "One thing I have learned is that children, whilst requiring discipline, also require to be loved. To be shown kindness and consideration, to be listened to, and to enjoy each day. Henry is about to start his letters today and I am certain that he shall do very well, simply because he knows that I do care for him a great deal already." She spread her hands, lifting both of her shoulders. "I do not know why he resides with you rather than with his own parents, but I *do* know that he feels lost, afraid, and alone."

"He does not reside with his parents because one has passed from this earth and the other has disappeared." Albina's heart slammed against her chest. Shock ran like ice through her veins, and she could not speak. "His mother passed away some years ago, only a few months after Henry was born." Lord Addenbrook spoke in clipped tones and without the smallest hint of emotion. "My brother did not remarry. In the years that followed, I believe he spent a good deal of time with Henry and was very fond of his son. A little over three months ago, my brother and Henry were due to come here to stay for a prolonged visit. When the carriage arrived, only Henry was inside." He blinked and looked away, clearly pushing back any flicker of emotion. "When I stepped out to greet them, I noticed that both the coachman and the footman were gone, which was most unusual. When my footman opened the carriage door, there was no sign of my brother – and Henry was asleep on the floor." Albina did not know what to say. The shock of hearing such a thing from him stole her ability to respond, leaving her mute with astonishment. When Lord Addenbrook glanced back at her, his expression was hard and cold. "Whenever I am in company with Henry, it reminds me of just how little I have managed to achieve in finding my brother."

Struggling to order her thoughts, Albina took in a long breath and attempted to nod.

"I am certain that you are doing all you can."

A hard laugh ripped from Lord Addenbrook's throat, but Albina did not understand the reasons for it – and Lord Addenbrook himself did not explain.

"You may return to your charge now, Miss Trean." He rose and Albina quickly followed suit, finding that her legs were a trifle wobbly. "I wanted you to be aware of the current situation so that, should Henry say anything to you about the matter, you will be able to respond with understanding."

Albina spread her hands.

"That is most considerate of you, Lord Addenbrook." She might not agree that his absence from the child's company was the best thing for both himself and Henry, but at least now she understood why. "I do hope that further inquiries bring you answers."

She said nothing more, but left the room with all swiftness, closing the door tightly behind her. Before she made her way to the schoolroom, however, she took just a few moments to gather herself. Her eyes closed and she put one hand out against the wall for support, pain rifling through her as she thought of all that young Henry had endured – and all that he had lost.

Mayhap he will tell me something of significance about what happened to his father. Her eyes opened and she slowly began to make her way back towards the schoolroom. *I doubt that he will have spoken openly to Lord Addenbrook, but if Henry comes to trust me then he may very well tell me something of importance. Something that could help determine the whereabouts of his father.* But then she recalled that Lord Addenbrook had spoken of Henry going to Eton and how that would take place in a few years' time – and her heart sank. Clearly, Lord Addenbrook did not think that he would ever be able to recover his brother alive. For whatever reason, he had determined that Henry would never again return to what had once been his home.

He believed that his brother was dead.

CHAPTER FIVE

*P*atrick glanced up at the clock and then set down his quill.

It's time.

Rising from his study chair, he made his way to the window and looked outside, waiting for Miss Trean and Henry to step out into the gardens. They did so at the same time every day and, for whatever reason, Patrick had found himself eager to watch them for a few minutes. He had told himself that it was simply due to his concern for his nephew, to make certain that Miss Trean was doing her duties well, but if he had to be entirely honest with himself, Patrick knew it was more than that. The governess' gentleness with Henry was a merit to her and yet the temerity with which she had spoken to him on various occasions ought to have detracted from his opinion of her character – but for whatever reason, it had not.

"There they are." Murmuring to himself, Patrick leaned a little closer to the window, watching Miss Trean as she took Henry's hand and walked with him towards the rose gardens. Henry, however, soon tugged his hand out of Miss Trean's and began to run, making the lady laugh and then call after him to be careful.

A smile spread, unbidden, across Patrick's face.

This was not as I had intended. The smile faded as he realized the truth. When Miss Trean had been sent for, he had expected that her arrival would grant him back the freedom he had been so desperately longing for. He did not want to even *think* about Henry and, in many regards, wanted to pretend that he did not have a nephew, did not have a small child residing with him who called him 'uncle'. Did not have a missing brother... Patrick wanted to return to a time when he did not have any other responsibilities besides those of a Marquess, back to when he had been able to write to his brother and have him respond.

Back to before he had lost him.

Patrick dropped his head and rubbed one hand over his eyes. His brother, James Dutton, had been missing for three months now and Patrick was quite at a loss as to what to do next. When that carriage had arrived with only Henry within, Patrick had not known what to do. It had only been on the advice of his butler that he had sent word to his brother's estate, informing the household of what had taken place. The servants there had searched for Dutton and Patrick had sent out various men to various places to find him, but it had been to no avail. And now, whilst some of his men were still out searching, seeking out even the smallest whisper of information that might be useful, nothing had given Patrick even the tiniest encouragement.

Aware of the heaviness growing in his soul, Patrick lifted his head and looked out into the gardens again. Miss Trean had taken Henry by both hands and was swinging him around and, even from behind the glass, Patrick could hear the screams of delight.

He smiled.

Then turned and scrubbed one hand over his face, removing that particular expression. He did not need to find himself caught up with the young lady. Yes, it was good that she had done so well with Henry thus far, but mayhap he was becoming a little distracted.

And that was not like him.

"She is a governess," he reminded himself aloud. "You are a Marquess. You ought not to be seeking out her company, nor watching her from the window. That is a little ridiculous."

Sitting down again in his chair, Patrick closed his eyes and rested his head back. The truth was, she brought a little light into his otherwise dark world. Yes, he paraded his wealth as best he could to others and the house parties declared his joviality and humor, but Patrick was aware that he used them to hide the pain he struggled with, the confusion that surrounded him over the loss of his brother. It was easier to pretend than to face the truth: he was failing Dutton.

A scratch at the door came and Patrick called the butler to enter.

"You have a visitor, my Lord."

"Oh?" Patrick arched one eyebrow, a little surprised to hear that someone had come to call. Perhaps it was Lord Newford come to gloat at the recent mishap, or Lord Hogarth deciding to come and steal some of Patrick's brandy. "Who is it?"

The butler came into the room and closed the door behind him.

"I believe it is the Earl of Kingston, my Lord."

Patrick frowned.

"I do not think I have ever been acquainted with such a gentleman."

"I do not believe you have, my Lord, no."

The butler stood by the door, waiting. Patrick's frown grew but he did not make an immediate decision. It was most unusual for a gentleman that had never been acquainted with him to suddenly decide to call, even if it *was* the summertime.

"Does he wish to see around the grounds and the house itself?"

Sometimes, there were those of lower social rank than he who called at the house so that they might be shown around it, since the estate was large and the house itself very well presented – but that usually only took place when Patrick was absent.

"Lord Kingston wished only to speak to you, my Lord."

All the more perplexed, Patrick shrugged and nodded.

"Very well. Have some refreshments sent."

The butler nodded and Patrick rose from his chair, ready to greet the gentleman. Quite why the man had arrived, Patrick did not know, and he was a little frustrated at being so interrupted. It was somewhat rude to arrive at the house of someone you had never met!

He did not have time to ponder this for long, for within one minute of the butler's departure, he returned again and stepped into Patrick's study.

"Lord Kingston, my Lord."

The butler inclined his head towards Patrick, then turned and gestured towards him, expecting Lord Kingston to step inside. Patrick studied the man who walked into the room and felt no sudden flicker of recognition. He did not know this gentleman at all.

"My most humble apologies for calling upon you in such a fashion, Lord Addenbrook." Lord Kingston stopped and bowed low, his dark hair falling forward over his eyes. "I know that we have never been acquainted but I have reason to call upon you without introduction."

"I see." Patrick gestured to the empty chairs near the fireplace and waited until Lord Kingston had sat down before he followed suit, sitting opposite the gentleman. "And what might those reasons be?" He did not wait for refreshments to arrive, did not engage in small, meaningless conversation but drove straight to the point of Lord Kingston's arrival. "What was it that you had to say to me that simply could not wait?"

Lord Kingston's eyes flared in surprise, but he did not protest.

"I have heard, Lord Addenbrook, that you have recently lost a brother." His mouth tugged to one side as he shook his head. "That is, I do not mean to say that you have had need to arrange a funeral, but rather that the man has disappeared from your sight." Patrick nodded slowly, frowning as he did so. It was, of course, to be known amongst society that Dutton had not been seen for some time and, given the way the town gossips would have clung to such news, it made sense that a great number of the *ton* would have heard of it. "You do not like to speak of such news, I am sure."

"No, I do not." His words were clipped, his voice low. "It is a difficult situation."

Lord Kingston nodded, opening his mouth to ask something more – only for the maid to tap at the door and then bring in a tray of refreshments. Patrick saw Lord Kingston's eyes widen at the selection brought to him and a tiny nudge of satisfaction pushed itself into his heart. Waiting until the maid had left the room, Patrick then gestured to the trays.

"Please, do help yourself."

Lord Kingston nodded, his eyes still a little wide.

"As I was saying, such a situation is very painful one and it is not something that I have any particular interest in discussing." Patrick cleared his throat, rose to his feet, and made his way across the room so that he might pour a measure of brandy for them both. "However, I must surmise that you have some particular reason to come here and begin to talk to me about this." One eyebrow lifted as he handed Lord Kingston back his glass. "Might I enquire as to what it is?"

The man took a sip of his brandy first before he replied, forcing Patrick to wait for a few moments longer, irritating him. Choosing not to return to his seat, Patrick wandered across the room and stood by the window, glancing down to see Miss Trean and Henry beginning to meander towards the house again. It seemed as though Henry's time to be out of doors was over for another day.

"I come to you, Lord Addenbrook, because there has come a very similar disappearance within my own sphere."

Patrick turned sharply, looking back at Lord Kingston with wide eyes.

"Indeed?"

The fellow nodded gravely, bringing his brandy to his lips again.

"I was about to become betrothed. The arrangements had been made between myself and her father and I was certain that the lady would accept me." Turning back to face the window, Patrick allowed Lord Kingston to keep speaking without interruption, choosing to watch Miss Trean as she walked back to the house. One hand was wrapped around Henry's shoulders and the boy leaned against her skirts, clearly exhausted. Patrick smiled. "However, the day that I was to propose, the lady was nowhere to be found! I received a frantically written note from her mother begging me to come to the house and aid them in their search – but thus far, they have never been able to discover her."

Miss Trean and Henry stepped inside, and Patrick let out a slow breath, quickly realizing that Lord Kingston had stopped speaking. Turning back towards him, he gave the man his full attention.

"You say your betrothed has gone from her parents' house?"

"Yes, that is it precisely!" Lord Kingston exclaimed. "But who has taken her, we cannot say. There is no trace of her anywhere in London – although we have been discreet with our inquiries, of course – and then when I heard that your brother had also been lost, I thought to come to see if you had any hint of where he might now be."

"In the hope that this would also lead to your betrothed?"

Nodding fervently, Lord Kingston closed his eyes tightly, perhaps fighting back the emotion that must now swamp him.

"That is exactly so. As I have said, there is no sign of her anywhere in London and I now fear what might have happened to her."

Patrick bit his lip. He did not want to sound cruel, but there was an obvious explanation that could be given.

"Might it be that the lady has eloped?" He saw the flash of anger in Lord Kingston's eyes and held up both hands. "I do not mean to upset you but if there was another –"

"There was not." Lord Kingston's voice was low, his

eyes hard. "Lady Albina had no interest in any other gentleman. Besides which, news of an elopement would be sent to the parents of such an unfortunate person before their return to society and, as yet, such news has not been received."

"And you would expect it to be?" Patrick tilted his head. "Is there a chance that the lady has not managed to wed the gentleman she hoped and has now found herself lost and alone in Scotland, waiting for someone to come to find her?"

Watching Lord Kingston carefully, Patrick was surprised when he dropped his head forward and ran one hand over his eyes. This was a greater display of emotion than he had expected.

"I do not think – I cannot believe that such a thing would take place." When he lifted his head, his dark eyes appeared all the heavier. "Lady Albina was not a young lady who gave her affections easily. I do not believe that she could be so disloyal *nor* so easily affected. She has a clear head, and her intentions are always precise. To be swayed by someone who, for whatever reason, could not ask her father's permission for her hand, seems entirely unthinkable. I do not believe that."

Patrick shrugged inwardly. Could a gentleman truly be so certain of a lady's intentions? He personally did not think so.

"There is no evidence that she left of her own accord, then?"

Lord Kingston shook his head.

"None of her clothes were packed, no personal items taken. No horse was gone, and her father's carriage was still where it had been left the previous evening. It appeared as though she had simply retired to bed one evening and then been left to waken elsewhere the following day – leaving me without my betrothed." Spreading his hands, his empty brandy glass still clasped in one of them, Lord Kingston's eyes fixed themselves to Patrick's. "I am at a loss. Her father is deeply upset and her mother distraught but, of course, they wish to hide this from the *ton* as best as they can, so that it does not immediately spread throughout London and indeed, all of England, that their daughter is gone. She will be quite ruined."

Patrick nodded slowly.

"That is understandable, certainly." A line formed between his brows as he wandered back towards his seat. "And they sent you here?"

"No, I came here of my own accord in the hope that you might have some light to shed on my current predicament. Your brother and my betrothed appear to have disappeared in much the same way, albeit in different circumstances."

This, Patrick considered, was not something he could ignore. Lord Kingston was quite correct, but there was nothing that Patrick could either suggest or advise that would be in any way encouraging.

"That may be so, Lord Kingston, but I cannot help you." Spreading out his hands wide, he shrugged. "I am quite at a loss."

Lord Kingston's eyes closed, and his shoulders slumped. "I see."

"My brother's absence is one of my great struggles," Patrick continued. "It has been three months since his disappearance, and I have not even the smallest hope of finding him. It is as though he simply disappeared into the fog and could not find his way back again."

Lord Kingston nodded but his mouth pulled into a flat line.

"I quite understand." His low voice told Patrick that he

felt a good deal more than he was able to express. "In my confused, convoluted thinking I had considered that they – whoever it is that has taken my betrothed – might first have taken your brother, for three months is not a particularly long length of time."

"But for what purpose?"

Throwing up his hands, Lord Kingston slumped back in his chair.

"I do not know."

Patrick hesitated. He was not inclined towards generosity but, for the first time, he was aware of a growing sense of understanding between them. Perhaps it would do him good to hear the precise details of Lord Kington's situation and Patrick could, thereafter, share the particulars of *his* difficulty. Would that bring any relief to them both?

"Are you staying nearby?"

Lord Kingston's eyes widened but he nodded.

"I have lodgings for the next day or so. It is much too far to return to London on the same day, so I thought to rest before doing so."

Nodding, Patrick paused, making certain within himself that this was what he wanted.

"I am to host a house party here that begins two days hence," he told his guest. "If you wish, you would be most welcome to join us. It is only for four days, but it would give us both plenty of opportunity to discuss our situations and to see if there is anything that might give either of us a little clarity."

"That is *most* generous of you."

Patrick smiled. There was a great deal of satisfaction in being so benevolent since it set him in a good light.

"But of course."

"I should be glad to accept. I will return to my lodgings

and send a letter at once to London, requesting a few of my things – and, of course, to know if there is any further information about where Lady Albina has gone."

It did not cross Patrick's mind to ask about the lady's appearance, her family or any other particulars. As far as he was concerned, this was an opportunity to discover if there was anything that Lord Kingston knew that could aid him, so he had very little interest in the lady herself.

"But of course."

Rising, he shook Lord Kingston's hand, accepted his further compliments, and then raised a hand in farewell as the gentleman took his leave.

His smile quickly faded as he reached for his brandy glass and threw back the rest in one large swallow. The reminder of his brother's absence was a difficult one, and Patrick struggled against the wave of shame that crashed up hard against him. He did not want to be pulled into the overwhelming sea of guilt, engulfed in it as it threatened to overpower him, and he fought hard against it.

I have done everything I can. Grimacing, he slammed the brandy glass down hard on the table. *But there is always the feeling that I should do more – even if I do not know what such a thing should be.*

Sighing heavily, Patrick rubbed one hand over his eyes. He would have to inform the staff that another guest was to join them for the house party which, no doubt, would cause something of an upset, but that could not be helped. His frown grew. He should also inform Miss Trean about the house party for he could not be certain that any of the staff had told her. Henry would have to be kept out of the way of the guests as much as possible although he did not want to restrict him entirely to the schoolroom. The thought of watching Miss Trean and Henry walking across the garden grounds pushed the frown away from his forehead and instead, made him smile. He would speak to Miss Trean as soon as was possible in the hope that, after their conversation, his smile would linger for a little longer than it did at present.

CHAPTER SIX

Albina rested her head back against the rocking chair and closed her eyes. Henry was wrapped in her arms, and she was struggling to keep her eyes open. Having always had the leisure of rising whenever she wished, she now found herself so very fatigued that it was almost impossible not to fall asleep whenever Henry did. Pushing her toes off the floor, Albina let the chair rock gently backward and forward as she cradled the child, feeling his head lolling on her shoulder.

A small smile crept across her lips as she let out a soft sigh. Henry had done so well with his letters these last two days but after their luncheon and their walk in the grounds, he was beginning to complain of weariness. So yesterday, Albina had simply offered to hold him tight while she rocked the chair for a short while – and both today and yesterday, Henry had been asleep in a matter of minutes.

Albina did not mind. She herself could do with a little additional rest. Having heard yet more scuffling sounds yesterday evening and even being woken by them during the night, Albina was weary. Her life here was very different to that of being Lady Albina, daughter of an Earl, but despite the rats, despite her altered situation, there were many things she had become grateful for – and one of them was Henry. Her eyes drifted closed and with the smile lingering on her lips, Albina fell asleep.

"Miss Trean?"

Waking with a start, Albina saw the concerned face of Miss Fullerton looking back at her. A little embarrassed, she shifted slightly in her chair, still holding Henry tight.

"Yes? Miss Fullerton, is it not?"

The young lady smiled.

"It is. I am companion to Lady Havisham."

Albina nodded, making sure to speak quietly.

"I remember."

"Lord Addenbrook begged me to come in search of you. It seems he wishes to speak to you."

Albina closed her eyes and tried to hide her frustration.

"I see."

"He thought to send a maid, but I offered to come to find you instead. I understand that there is no urgency to his request, but he has asked you to join him in the drawing-room when your duties with Henry come to an end for the day. After dinner has been served."

Albina tried to smile, but butterflies poured into her stomach, sending her heart to slam hard against her chest.

"Of course."

Miss Fullerton nodded and made to take a step back, only to smile down at Henry.

"He is peaceful with you."

"He is heavy!" Albina murmured, making Miss Fullerton laugh softly. "But yes, I shall not move until he awakens which will not be too long from now, I am sure."

Miss Fullerton's smile lingered.

"There was a time when I was destined to be a governess, but I took a position as companion instead. Sometimes I do wonder if I made the correct choice."

Albina returned the lady's smile.

"I think we must do what we can out of whatever situation presents itself to us."

The young lady sighed audibly, her shoulders dropping.

"That is true indeed."

Albina opened her mouth to ask her something more, only for Henry to shift gently, his mouth opening and closing as if he intended to speak but had not managed to do so.

"Do excuse me."

Miss Fullerton made her way to the door, leaving Albina and Henry to themselves. Albina sighed and rested her head back again although she did not close her eyes. That was one of the few times that anyone had spoken to her with any sort of kindness. She did not eat her meals with the servants but took them in the schoolroom, for her societal status was higher than theirs and Albina knew from Mrs. Stanley that she would not be welcomed. Nor was she welcomed to dine with the master and his guests, for her position as Miss Trean had pushed her a little lower in society.

Silently, Albina wondered what it must be like for someone to live as a companion. Was her life at present much the same as Miss Fullerton? Did Miss Fullerton struggle with the quiet silence that so often wrapped itself around Albina's shoulders? The loneliness had become a part of her, for her life as a governess was something of a solitary existence, but Albina considered that she was, in fact, a little used to such a way of living. When at home, her mother had always been occupied with some matter or resting when she felt fatigued, whilst her father had been kept busy with estate matters. *At least there I had a great many things to distract me.* Henry shifted in his sleep and Albina smiled to herself. *Although Henry is the greatest distraction here, certainly!* Biting her lip, Albina wondered if she would have the boldness to ask Lord Addenbrook if she could have a book from his library. Without anything to read aside from Henry's schoolbooks, she was a trifle bereft of amusements.

Why does he wish to see me?

The question did not have any obvious nor easy answer and Albina tried to tell herself that she need not worry about anything. After what Lord Addenbrook had told her about his brother, surely he would not be eager to remove her from her position and send her away? Albina now considered that she was a little more secure here and that Lord Addenbrook mayhap trusted Henry in her care without reserve – but then again, she did not know the gentleman very well at all. Her teeth worried her lip as she thought, her eyes roving around the room.

"Are you sad, Miss Trean?"

Henry's sleepy voice made Albina glance down at him quickly, seeing the way his hazel eyes searched hers.

"I am not sad, no." When he sat up, she brushed his damp hair back from his forehead. "Did you have a bad dream?"

Henry shook his head but did not smile.

"My father was sad."

Every part of Albina's frame tensed but she did not grasp Henry's hand hard nor demand that he tell her everything at once. Instead, she simply smiled softly, tilted her head, and looked back at him.

"Is that so? What was he sad about?"

"He did not have enough coin."

Albina blinked but again, forced herself not to react with any sort of fervor for fear that it would push Henry away from her.

"Oh?"

"I do not know why."

"Then how do you know that he did not have enough coin? Was there something that he said to you?"

Albina kept her voice gentle, but Henry frowned and pushed himself off her knee.

"He did not say anything to me. I should not have listened, but I did."

"You listened to him talking to someone else?"

Henry nodded, his mouth a little pursed and his head lowered as if he was ashamed.

"You are right that you should not have listened. But what was it that you heard your father say? Just that he did not have the coin that was needed?"

The small boy mumbled something, and Albina reached out one gentle finger to tilt up his chin. When his eyes finally met hers, she saw that there were tears glistening there, and her heart squeezed with pain for him.

"Henry?"

He nodded.

"Do you know who he spoke to?"

Shaking his head, Henry rubbed at his nose with one hand.

"I don't remember."

This came out as something of a wail and Albina quickly wrapped him in her arms, holding him tightly.

"Thank you for telling me, Henry." She waited, wondering if he was going to start sobbing but his small frame did not begin to shake although he rubbed at his eyes with one hand. "You need not worry any longer. I know that you should not have been listening but what you have told me might be very helpful." She smiled down into Henry's face as he tipped his chin up and frowned as if he didn't quite believe her. "If you remember anything else, will you please tell me?" Henry nodded, his gaze falling away. "Thank you. Now, we must make certain that you are ready for dinner. Your hair will need to be brushed!"

Ignoring his protests, Albina rose from her rocking chair and taking the reluctant child by the hand, led him from the nursery and back into his bedchamber.

She had a good deal to tell Lord Addenbrook.

～

"Come in."

Albina took in a deep breath and then pushed open the door. It was already beginning to grow dark and many candles were lit. Lord Addenbrook was bent over his study desk, writing something at great speed, his quill scratching the paper. He did not say another word to her but gestured for her to come closer. Albina, who had been growing steadily more anxious for the last hour, did as she was bade and then waited, her hands clasped tightly in front of her.

"Miss Trean." Lord Addenbrook set down the quill with a sigh of relief and then sanded his letter before folding and sealing it. "I have something to speak to you about. I should have, mayhap, done so a little earlier but I did not." He shrugged as though that particular oversight did not matter. "Please, do be seated."

Albina tried to swallow past the lump in her throat, but she did not quite manage to remove it entirely. There was something rather intimidating about being in Lord Addenbrook's presence – whether it came from the fact that he could remove her from her position here and, unwittingly, send her back to her parents and Lord Kingston, she could not say, but there was something about the way he looked at her that had her all of a tremble.

Lord Addenbrook rose from his desk and, much to Albina's shock, began to untie his cravat. He flung it haphazardly on his desk and came towards her, one button now completely undone at the top of his shirt.

Fear began to curl within her stomach. Was he about to attempt to take advantage of her? Had this all been a ruse? With a sudden rush of awareness at just how very alone and vulnerable she was at present, Albina's hands clenched tightly into fists.

But then, Lord Addenbrook fell back into a chair opposite her and let out a heavy sigh. Clearly, he was *not* about to harm her, but was merely disinclined towards keeping his formal dress in front of a mere governess. A small, flickering heat began to burn in her chest and Albina's cheeks colored a gentle pink.

"I am to have a house party, Miss Trean."

Albina blinked.

This is all he wished to tell me?

"I should like you to make certain that Henry has no part in this endeavor. There will be a number of guests – one only just added to the party, in fact – and should not be particularly pleased if he were to disrupt it in any way." Pushing himself up in his chair, he lifted one shoulder. "I do not want my guests to know that I have a nephew currently residing in my house, Miss Trean. You may think poorly of me for that if you wish, but that is what I desire."

The tension which had run through her only a few

seconds ago lingered still, and it took her a few moments to reply.

"I understand, my Lord. When do they arrive?"

Grimacing, Lord Addenbrook's eyes darkened as they swept over her.

"In two days' time, in the late afternoon." A small sigh fell from his lips. "Alas, I fear that you *do* think poorly of me."

Albina took in a deep breath.

"I do not know why my opinion should matter, my Lord," she answered, speaking with more boldness than any other governess might. "I will do as you ask and make certain that Henry is not seen by any of the guests."

"I should not like you to be forced to hide in the schoolroom and nursery for these four days, however." Lord Addenbrook spoke quickly as if he wanted to make amends for the demands which he had just placed on her. "The guests will not rise early. In fact, I should not imagine that any would rise before luncheon!" A small smile tugged at his mouth and Albina could not help but smile, knowing full well that this was often the case with those in the *ton*. "If you wished to take your walk with Henry during the morning hours, then that would be acceptable."

It would mean a change to her current plan with Henry, but Albina did not mind. She had not realized it at first, but now slowly began to think of what it would have been like should Lord Addenbrook have demanded that *she* come to present Henry to the guests when they arrived. She did not know who it was that he had invited but what if one of them had recognized her? Then all would have failed, and she would have been forced to return home and into whatever circumstance was waiting for her. Relief coursed through her, and she made to rise from her chair, glad now that she would have cause to stay away from Lord Addenbrook's guests. Lord Addenbrook had, without realizing it, saved her from what could have been a very difficult situation indeed.

"Oh, I quite forgot." Seeing Lord Addenbrook's lifted brow, Albina flushed gently but remained in her chair. "Henry spoke of his father."

In an instant, Lord Addenbrook's expression changed. He pushed himself forward, no longer reclining back in his chair, and put his elbows on his knees, his hands clasped tightly together. His eyes swirled with gold and green, his mouth pulling into a flat line.

"What did he say?"

Quickly, Albina related what Henry had told her, seeing Lord Addenbrook close his eyes once she had reached the end.

"This was my very great concern," he breathed, closing his eyes and shaking his head. "I *told* him that I...."

Dropping his head forward, he pushed one hand through his hair but remained in that position for a few seconds.

Albina's heart flooded with sympathy, and she was half out of her chair before she realized what she was doing.

Sit down, Albina.

It was too late. Lord Addenbrook lifted his head to look at her and Albina, now standing in front of him, tried to smile.

"I – I should take my leave now, my Lord." She did not want him to know that her instinct had been to reach out to him, to take his hand and to press it gently by way of encouragement. "Pray excuse me."

A paleness was in his cheeks which had not been there before.

"My brother is something of a gambler, Miss Trean. I have begged him many a time to stop doing such a thing, aware that his fortune was dwindling, but he struggled to do so. I am afraid now that his debts will have become so great that he dared not speak of them to me and thus, *that* is why he is gone from my company."

Albina's shoulders dropped. She could not leave now, not when he spoke with such openness. Silently, she wondered if Lord Addenbrook had spoken of such a thing to anyone else, or if that was such a private matter – and such a shameful one – that it would be kept from as many of the *ton* as possible.

"You think that he has been taken by those who demanded he repay his debts?"

Perching on a smaller chair which was a little closer to Lord Addenbrook, she waited for him to reply. Either he would do so without hesitation, or he would shake his head and bring the conversation to a close.

Lord Addenbrook groaned aloud, dropped his head, and ran both hands through his hair.

"Miss Trean, you will not be surprised, I think, when I tell you that I have a great deal of wealth." His voice was muffled, hidden by his arms as his head lowered further still. "I am much inclined towards pride. I do not hide from that. It brings me a great deal of satisfaction to show such wealth to those around me, whether they approve of my doing so or not." His head lifted and his eyes shot straight to hers, pinning her in place. "Did my brother choose not to speak to me about his debts because of my arrogance?"

It was a question that Albina could not answer. Pressing her lips tight together, she hesitated as she considered, wondering what it was that she might say. This was not a situation she had ever found herself in before for, as Lady

Albina, she had never had deep conversations with any gentleman. It had always been simple, uninvolved discussion whereas now, in her role as governess, she was being drawn into a situation that she did not understand and could not speak into.

"Do you believe that your brother has been taken by those he owes money to, my Lord?"

It was the second time she had asked such a question, but Lord Addenbrook, as yet, had not answered it. Grimacing, he shook his head tightly.

"I cannot tell, Miss Trean." There was a thickness to his voice now, one which hid what he truly felt at that moment. "It may be that my brother has given me Henry to care for whilst he attempts to find a way to pay for his debts." Running one hand across his forehead, Albina heard his long, prolonged sigh of frustration. "If I could only beg of him to tell me of his present circumstances, then –"

"Could you not find out from his man of business what debts your brother might owe?" Albina had not meant to interrupt him, but the idea had flung itself into her mind and needed to be spoken just as soon as was possible. "That way, you would have the names of those concerned and could, if you wished, pay the debts owed. That way, your brother would no longer have to worry about his debts, at least."

Lord Addenbrook blinked. His eyes rounded as he stared back at her and then, after a few moments, he began to laugh.

Albina flushed with embarrassment and dropped her head. Clearly, she had made some sort of mistake.

"No, Miss Trean, do not look so!"

Before she could react or respond, Lord Addenbrook

was out of his chair and had taken her hand, pressing it tightly.

"I do not laugh at your suggestion, but rather that I, who have been thinking on this matter for some time, have never even *thought* of such a thing." He pressed her hand again. "It is not that I mock you, Miss Trean, but rather that I find myself to be a little ridiculous in my lack of wisdom."

She lifted her head and looked up into his face. Lord Addenbrook's expression was sincere, for his eyes were searching her face and his lips curved into a soft smile.

Her heart quickened. His hand was warm on hers and for the first time, a great swell of sympathy crashed over her.

"Thank you."

Her voice was a little wobbly, which only made Albina's embarrassment grow all the more, but Lord Addenbrook did not appear to notice.

"That is a very wise thought, Miss Trean, and one I ought to have thought of myself. I shall write to my brother's man of business at once and mayhap I shall have some news to tell Lord Kingston when he arrives!"

Albina stilled. Ice was filling her, running from her toes to the top of her head at the sound of Lord Kingston's name. She could not move. Lord Addenbrook was still speaking but she heard none of it. The same words ran through her mind over and over again, screaming at her until she shuddered.

Lord Kingston was coming.

CHAPTER SEVEN

"And what a very pleasant aspect one has approaching your exceptional manor house, Lord Addenbrook."

Patrick waited for the familiar swell of satisfaction to rise up in his chest but much to his surprise, it did not appear. Lady Gower looked at him curiously and it took Patrick a moment to respond.

"Yes, yes, I am glad you found it pleasant." He saw the quick exchange of looks between Lady Gower and her daughter and became quickly aware of how poorly he had managed to respond to her remark. "I do hope you will enjoy your time here. I have one further guest soon to arrive – one Lord Kingston."

"Oh!" Miss Miller's eyes flared. "I have heard of him, although I am not acquainted. Is he not the Earl of Kingston?"

"The very same."

Lady Gower sniffed and lifted her chin.

"I have heard that he has recently lost the affection of one Lady Albina," she told them both, although Patrick found himself listening with far more interest than he had expected. "I was certain that they would soon be betrothed but nothing has been announced and, indeed, I have seen Lord Kingston in London many times of late but she has never been in his company."

Patrick gave her a small smile whilst inwardly frustrated on Lord Kingston's behalf. There was a reason that Lady Gower had not seen Lady Albina in Lord Kingston's company but, of course, that reason could not easily be explained.

"I have heard that Lord Kingston is not the very best of gentlemen."

"That is enough," Lady Gower put in, silencing her daughter immediately. Miss Miller dropped her head but not before Patrick saw the red flush in her cheeks. He did not dismiss her comment, however, but pushed it to the back of his mind.

"I do not know Lord Kingston particularly well, but I thought there was no reason not to have him join us," he told them both, as Lady Gower nodded. "I am certain we shall all have the very best of parties and that you will find the company to be quite exceptional."

Excusing himself, he rose from his chair and went to speak to another guest whilst still quietly thinking about what Miss Miller had said of Lord Kingston before her mother had silenced her on the subject. After all, given that he was not well acquainted with the gentleman, it was wise to consider what others thought of him. It would determine whether or not he would want to continue with such an acquaintance.

Joining a conversation with Lady Foster, Lord Hogarth, and one of Lady Foster's elegant daughters, Patrick enquired after everyone's health, welcomed them to his home, and found himself wondering why he did not feel as proud of his current situation as he usually did. This was usually the time in his house party where he felt the greatest satisfaction when his guests were wandering around his manor house and exclaiming over the various aspects of his grand abode. Now, however, he found that his mind was somewhat distracted.

But it was not thoughts of Lord Kingston which clouded his mind. It was not the house party and his guests. It was not even his brother who pulled at his thoughts. Instead, it was none other than Miss Trean who lingered there.

Why am I thinking about the governess when I ought to be considering nothing other than my guests?

Patrick turned to pour himself another brandy and then offered one to Lord Hogarth, allowing the group's conversation to flow around him. The time he had shared with Miss Trean had not left him. It had been somewhat significant, given that he had never spoken of his brother, nor the feelings which pulled at his heart, to anyone.

But Miss Trean's eyes had been so gentle and her presence so much of a comfort that it felt as though he had been compelled into speech. He had not been embarrassed to speak in such a way, had not found himself ashamed of expressing the truth of his feelings to her. And the way that she had given him a way forward had astonished him. She had seen into the situation in a way that he had never been able to do and had made the suggestion of writing to his brother's man of business so that any debts might soon be made known. In three months of his brother's absence, Patrick had never thought of such a thing himself and yet Miss Trean, with only a few minutes of consideration, had found a way to help him.

She was most unusual.

"I did hear that you had a small boy running wild through your house, Lord Addenbrook."

Pulled back from his thoughts, Patrick forced a smile to his face as Lady Violet looked at him with one gently lifted eyebrow.

"Indeed, Lady Violet. You have heard correctly, but you need not concern yourself that such a creature will disturb our endeavor here for these few days." He did not give any explanation to the young lady but quickly turned the conversation to something else. "Now do tell me of London, Lady Violet. How is it that you have not yet found a suitor? I am certain that all the gentlemen of London must be jostling for even a minute of your attention."

The flattery worked for both mother and daughter and soon Lady Violet and Lady Foster were both talking of London and all the very pleasant company that they had each enjoyed there. Patrick flicked a grin towards Lord Hogarth who was watching Lady Violet intently. His friend quickly returned it and soon drew himself into direct conversation with Lady Violet, allowing Patrick to excuse himself.

He did not linger with his guests but, claiming that he had to make certain that all was well and suitably prepared for them, he went from the drawing-room and out into the long hallway, making his way past the front door of the house – just as it opened.

Caught by surprise, he stopped dead.

"Miss Trean!" A small flare of annoyance brought his brows low over his eyes. "Did I not make myself quite plain? Henry is not to be –" He stopped, his attention caught by Henry who leaned against Miss Trean, his arms around her skirts. He did not look up at Patrick but kept his head bent, making Patrick's frustration change quickly into guilt, stabbing hard through his heart. He did not want the child to be afraid of him, but it was not as though he had made any effort to encourage the boy. Clearing his throat, he tried to speak again with a little more calmness in his voice. "Do excuse me for interrupting you both. Henry, did you enjoy your walk out of doors?"

His nephew lifted his head briefly, his eyes wide as he looked back at Patrick. Miss Trean patted the top of his head gently and Henry eventually nodded.

"That is good." Patrick smiled, finding himself relieved when Henry lifted his head a little more and eventually began to step a little bit away from Miss Trean. "I am sorry I spoke crossly. That was not good, and I shall not do it again. Will that please you?" Henry blinked, nodded and then finally, smiled. "Good, then I shall endeavor to be just as happy and as friendly as you."

Miss Trean touched the boy's shoulder.

"Here, Henry, go with Jean." Miss Trean ushered him towards a maid that Patrick had not even noticed step into the hallway and then untied her bonnet ribbons, removing it and holding it in her hand. "I shall come up to the nursery in a few moments."

Patrick watched the small boy take the maid's hand and walk away with her, his head turning so that he might glance back at Miss Trean. Taking a deep breath and making sure to speak without any hint of anger, he took a step closer to the governess.

"As I was saying, Miss Trean, I was certain that I made myself quite clear."

The lady's hands went straight to her hips.

"You told me plainly that your guests would be arriving in the late afternoon, Lord Addenbrook." Her obvious frustration had Patrick stuttering to a stop, having been quite ready to continue on with his frustrations. "I thought I should walk out with Henry after luncheon so that we would not disturb your guests! I have done only as you instructed and now you attempt to blame me?"

Throwing up her hands, she made to turn and spin away from him but Patrick, before he knew what he was doing, had reached out and caught her hand. Miss Trean, surprised by his hand on hers, stumbled and Patrick caught her as she fell against his chest.

Surprise came first. It spread out across his chest as he looked down at Miss Trean, only just realizing for the first time the depths in her blue eyes. She blinked, her mouth a little ajar with surprise and one hand resting against his chest. Silence spread out around them, capturing them together in this one moment. Neither of them moved, but Patrick was all too aware of a steadily growing heat that began to burn in the middle of his chest, right where Miss Trean was against him.

She moved first.

"I – I do apologize." Turning all about her, she stepped back and then picked up her bonnet which Patrick had not even noticed had fallen from her hand. "I shall, of course, make certain that both myself and Henry do not become known to any of your guests." Taking in a deep breath that lifted her shoulders and sent a calmness into the rolling seas in her eyes, Miss Trean looked directly into his face. "I apologize for speaking out of turn, my Lord. You are, of course, quite correct."

"No, I am not." Patrick moved closer, still astonished not only by what he had done but by what he had felt. "I do not recall speaking exactly to you about what time the guests would arrive but that in itself is a failure on my part. I spoke rashly and without consideration." His hand reached out towards her, but Patrick pulled it back with an effort, knowing he had no right nor need to take her hand, even though the desire to do so was very strong indeed. "Do not apologize, Miss Trean. I will make certain that, one way or another, you remain informed about all the particulars as regards the guests."

"That is most kind of you." She bit her lip, as if she were about to say something more, then turned her head away, leaving Patrick suddenly desperate to find out what it was she had been going to say.

Someone coughed behind him, and Patrick turned.

"Yes?"

The butler came a little closer, but Patrick did not move away from Miss Trean.

"My Lord, I believe another carriage has just arrived. Is this your final guest?"

A long sigh of frustration ripped from Patrick's mouth. It was not that he did not want to see or spend time with his guests but more than, at the present time, he wanted very much just to be with Miss Trean and converse only with her – in the hope that he might somehow be able to discover a little more about what it was he felt at present since it was all so very strange.

"It will be Lord Kingston."

A small exclamation came from Miss Trean and Patrick turned swiftly, seeing the paleness sweep into her cheeks. Her eyes met his, but she quickly began to back away, one hand held up, palm out, towards him.

"Forgive me, I should not be holding you back from your guests, Lord Addenbrook. Pray excuse me."

The realization that she was afraid of overstepping the clear boundary he had just set down for the second time made Patrick's heart sink. He did not want her to be afraid of him nor worry that there would be particular consequences for her should she make any sort of mistake, but yet that appeared to be the impression he was giving her.

And I will not see her for the next few days. Even though she will be living in my house and spending all of her time with my nephew. That thought sent his heart lurching after her, as if it yearned to be where she was instead of greeting Lord Kingston and spending time with his guests. *I could always go to see Henry. I could....*

Patrick shook his head to himself and pinched the bridge of his nose. He would not pretend. The fact was, he was beginning to realize that the way Henry viewed him was not in a pleasant light and that was something that Patrick wished to change – but perhaps now was not the time for such a thing. Perhaps now he ought to think solely about his guests and his house party and make sure that they all took with them a great appreciation for his home, his possessions, and his wealth so that, in turn, they would be reminded of his status and his title and just how grateful they should be that he was in their acquaintance – because that was what he wanted - wasn't it?

CHAPTER EIGHT

"My uncle does not wish to see me?"

"Your uncle is very busy with his guests." Albina pulled up the blankets a little more around Henry. "But you know that he cares for you."

"He is often very angry with me."

Albina hesitated before she answered, wanting to do justice both to Lord Addenbrook and to Henry.

"I do not believe that you always behaved well, however. There was cause for him to be cross with you." Seeing the boy frown, Albina continued to smooth the blankets. "But he should not have shouted so. You must trust me when I tell you that your uncle has a great affection for you, my dear. You are his nephew after all!"

"But I think that –"

"And now it is time for you to go to sleep." Albina interrupted, smiling down at him softly. "We can discuss your uncle a little more in the morning if you wish." Leaning forward, she brushed a kiss across Henry's cheek. The boy was very tired, and Albina was sure that he would fall into a deep sleep very soon. It had been an enjoyable day although, as Albina closed the door, she had to admit to herself that she was very worried indeed about residing in the same house as Lord Kingston. She had not heard him and certainly had not seen him but there was a prickling awareness of his presence. The knot of fear had tightened with every hour that had passed during the afternoon and evening and even now, Albina was aware of it tugging tighter still.

She did not think that she would be able to sleep. No doubt the creaks and scuffles coming from the walls of her room would keep her awake and she would then simply lie there, unable to close her eyes for fear that a rat would leap up onto her bed and onto her chest, Albina did not think that she would have a restful night. Her thoughts were already plagued, her mind whirring as she considered the fact that Lord Kingston was present in the house. It was just as well that the Marquess had insisted that Henry stay out of sight during the house party, else she might well have found herself in an inextricable situation.

"Miss Trean?"

Albina turned as she stood at the door.

"Yes?"

Henry's voice was soft, already tinged with sleep.

"My father will come to say good night to me, won't he?"

Her eyes slid closed as an ache pounded through her heart.

"We must both hope that he will be able to do so one day, Henry."

"I know that he will come." The boy yawned and a small, sad smile pulled at Albina's lips. "He will come in and kiss my cheek and say that he will come again tomorrow."

Albina walked back across the room, bent down, and kissed the small boy's cheek.

"One day, I hope, he will do just as I have done."

Smiling at the way his eyes fluttered closed, she smoothed his blankets and then returned to the door. Henry's breathing was already slow and deep, and Albina crept out of the room, wishing desperately that she could make Henry's request come true.

Maybe I should speak to Lord Addenbrook to see if he has received a reply to his letter. Closing the door carefully behind her, Albina leaned back against it and shut her eyes. *No, that would be foolish. He has enough to consider at present already.*

If there was anything of significance, she had to trust that Lord Addenbrook would inform her of it. Whilst he clearly did not want Henry's presence to interrupt the house party, Albina believed that he had the boy's best interests at heart. There was definitely upset – perhaps even anger – within him, over the fact that he had not yet been able to find his brother. Perhaps in seeing Henry, Lord Addenbrook was overcome with such emotions and thus did not want to spend much time with his nephew to avoid such feelings.

Pushing herself away from the door, Albina walked towards her bedchamber, passing the schoolroom as she went.

Something caught in her peripheral vision, and she stepped back, her brow furrowing – just as the door flew open and someone – Albina did not recognize their face – rushed from it. His shoulder caught hers and she staggered back, hitting her head hard against the wall. Slumping down against that wall with one hand going to her head, Albina let out a moan of pain as sparks flew in her vision.

Nobody heard her.

With no maids or footmen nearby, Albina was left to herself, struggling against the throbbing in her head. Blinking rapidly, her breathing a little ragged, she somehow managed to pull herself to standing, leaning heavily against the wall with one hand for support.

When she took her hand away, it was red with blood.

Even the sight made her head spin, but Albina forced herself to take one step forward and then the next. Quite how she made it down the staircase, she did not know, for her vision was blurred and the only sound she could hear was the thunderous pounding in her head.

"Miss Trean?"

A voice sounded very close to her, and Albina winced, closing her eyes tightly.

"Is there a reason that you are down from the nursery? Does not Henry require you?"

Albina, her hand still clamped to her head, tried to answer but her words were slightly slurred.

"He is asleep and will not wake until morning."

It was Lord Addenbrook, she realized. Managing to open her eyes, she saw him take a step back, his expression one of shock.

"Miss Trean." His voice was firmer now. "I will not abide you imbibing whilst you are here. Even if Henry is abed, that is no excuse for such a thing. I–"

It took Albina a moment to realize that the moan had come from her own lips. The air around her grew thin, her eyes closed of their own accord, and she tried to steady herself on something – anything – and her hand dropped from her head.

She did not hear Lord Addenbrook's swift intake of breath. She did not feel his arms around her, catching her as she fell and lifting her as he carried her to the library. The pain, for the moment, was quite gone as darkness overtook her and carried her away, her head lolling back and her body limp in Lord Addenbrook's arms.

"Miss Trean?"

Albina turned her head sharply and then wished she had not done so, for her head exploded with agony. She had revived a little over an hour ago and had been left in the capable hands of the maid and the housekeeper who had appeared to be rather concerned over her condition. However, with a little rest and a good deal of sweet tea, Albina now was now much recovered.

"Lord Addenbrook."

Albina made to move from her slightly reclined position, thinking that he had come to remove her from the library, but Lord Addenbrook quickly hurried towards her, his hands outstretched as though he intended to physically prevent such a thing.

"No, pray do not move." His hand rested on her shoulder and Albina settled back against the cushions, a little embarrassed at the situation. "Are you quite all right?"

"My head aches, but I am not at all close to fainting, as I once was." She tried to smile, but Lord Addenbrook's face remained set, filled with concern. "Thank you, my Lord, for your help. I will not intrude on your time any further."

Despite his closeness, she sat up carefully until she was in a seated position, smoothing her skirts over her knees. The pain in her head had lessened somewhat, but she was still very weary and the ache in her skull was pushing down into her neck and back. The only thing she wanted to do was retire so that she could sleep and, hopefully, recover. She would have to make certain to return to her room without delay and with the hope that none of the guests – particularly Lord Kingston – were nearby.

"Pray, stay for a few moments, until your color has improved." Lord Addenbrook sat down but it was only on the edge of the seat, his hands clasped, his elbows resting on his knees and his brows low over his eyes. "Can I have the maid bring you something more to drink? Tea? Mayhap a brandy?"

She shook her head, then winced.

"No, I am quite all right. I thank you."

"Might I ask what happened? Did you have some sort of fall?"

Albina hesitated. She did not want to bring any blame on any of the staff, but she also considered it important to inform Lord Addenbrook about what had occurred. The strength of the person who had pushed back against her, as well as their height, made her quite certain that it was a man rather than a woman who had collided with her.

"I had finished settling Henry in his bed and thought to retire early myself, as I have already prepared for the morrow. However, as I was making my way to my bedchamber, the door to the schoolroom opened and a man came out hurriedly, knocking into me." Dropping her eyes to the floor, she swallowed hard. "I was thrown back against the wall and hit my head."

"This man must have been in some haste."

She nodded.

"I suppose so."

Lord Addenbrook ran his fingers across his chin.

"Did you see who it was? Is it someone that you have seen before?"

"I did not have the opportunity to see who it was, my Lord." Albina spread her hands. "I cannot say whether or not it was someone I have already seen in your household." *It would not have been Lord Kingston, even though my heart is determined to push such a thought into my mind.* She drew in a deep breath, closing her eyes for a moment. "But for whatever reason, such a person was in the schoolroom, which is most unusual. And they did not stop after colliding with me – they simply continued, leaving me there."

Lord Addenbrook's lips bunched.

"That is, as you have said, *most* unusual. It is a pity that you did not get a closer look at the fellow." His eyes caught hers. "No-one ought to have been upstairs in the schoolroom, however. I will send someone to make certain that nothing has been disturbed and that the room is quite secure for you and Henry. You must inform me at once if such a thing ever happens again." She nodded, lowering her eyes. He was being very kind, and Albina certainly appreciated his reassurance. "I must also apologize for accusing you of imbibing, Miss Trean. That was inappropriate and I should not have thought such a thing of you."

His voice had softened, and Albina's heart quickened just a little. When she dared bring her eyes to his, there was a gentleness about them that made her heart race even more.

"I will accompany you to–"

There was a tap on the door before Lord Addenbrook could finish and, upon Lord Addenbrook's direction, the butler stepped in.

"My Lord, the guests are currently waiting for your direction."

Lord Addenbrook closed his eyes and let out a huff of breath.

"Very well."

Rising, he held out one hand towards Albina who, a little astonished, looked at it for a few seconds before realizing what she was meant to do.

Her hand touched his and something ignited in her core. Uncertain with what to do with such a sensation and afraid that he would see it in her eyes, Albina quickly lowered her gaze to the floor and rose to her feet, staggering forward a little as stars began to blur her vision.

"You need to rest." Lord Addenbrook's hand was tight on hers, his other hand slipping around her waist for a moment. "I will accompany you to your bedchamber."

Albina wanted to protest that she did not need him to assist her, and that she would be more than able to climb the staircase herself, but sense told her that she would be wise just to accept his help.

"I thank you. You are most kind."

"My Lord." The butler frowned, his gaze darting towards Albina for a moment. "Your guests. Is there anything required?"

Lord Addenbrook's head twisted towards him.

"I will be with them shortly. Miss Trean requires assistance after that dreadful incident and I must make certain that both she and Henry are safe for the remainder of the evening."

The butler did not protest, and Albina flushed, aware that Lord Addenbrook was putting her needs first before his guests.

"I do not wish to make any sort of difficulty, my Lord. I am sure that –"

"No. I will accompany you. Come, Miss Trean."

Without saying anything further, Lord Addenbrook walked towards the door which the butler obligingly opened for them. Albina walked alongside him, her face hot, but her heart filled with gratitude at his concern and his willingness to both help her and make certain that she was quite safe. This was more than she had expected from him. His nearness, however, sent all manner of sensations through her – sensations that she was not quite able to sort out and certainly unable to remove. They grew all the more as his hand supported her around her waist, his other hand still holding hers as they ascended the stairs.

"Do you require a maid?"

Albina smiled, grateful for the candles that now lit the hallway towards her bedchamber and towards Henry's. She would not have to stand here alone with him in the dark.

"No, I thank you."

"If there is anything that you require – or if you are too unwell come the morning – then you are to rest, and I will make certain that a maid takes on your responsibilities. You are not to worry, Miss Trean."

"You are most generous, Lord Addenbrook."

His hand was still tight on her own and a sensation of creeping warmth up her arm made Albina's face burn. She could only pray that he would not see her red face in the dim candlelight. Her eyes dropped to their joined hands, just as Lord Addenbrook looked down also. When he lifted his head, their eyes met and, with a clearing of his throat, Lord Addenbrook released her hand.

"I shall inform you at once if there is any need for change in Henry's care, although I am determined to make certain I am present with him as I usually am."

Lord Addenbrook's grin flashed white in the dim light.

"You are nothing if not determined, Miss Trean." His smile faded. "But I am certain that Henry will appreciate such determination a great deal."

There was nothing she could say in response to this. Hearing the edge of weariness in his voice, Albina stepped back.

"I should allow you to return to your guests." She bobbed a curtsey. "Thank you, Lord Addenbrook. You have been very kind to me."

"But of course." The firmness had returned to his voice and to his stature and, with a snap of his heels, he inclined his head just a little, as if he knew, somehow, that she was a lady rather than just a governess. "Good evening, Miss Trean, and I hope that you recover soon."

Albina could not help but watch him depart, her eyes fixed to his back and her heart fluttering wildly.

"Good night, Lord Addenbrook."

CHAPTER NINE

"And whilst you will, of course, see the many portraits from my family line, you will also find a good number of paintings from various artists that I admire." Patrick spread out his arms towards the hallway and heard the murmurs from his guests, just as he had expected. He waited expectantly for the sense of importance to swell in his chest, for the pride to lift his chin... but none came. Instead, he felt nothing. There was a dullness there, resting deep within him that seemed to steal every other sensation away. A frown chased down his brow. This was not what he had expected. "My most recent purchase you will find hanging here."

"Is that the one by Turner?"

Patrick glanced sharply at Lord Hogarth who, in his slightly befuddled state given the amount he had imbibed last evening, appeared to have forgotten what had happened to the Turner painting.

"No, it is not," he replied, a trifle coolly. "It is a Bernini."

Another few murmurings and Patrick tried to smile but instead, his lips dropped into a flat line. He was gaining very little enjoyment from this, and such a thing had never occurred before. This was meant to be the time when he felt the greatest amount of satisfaction, when his situation as the wealthiest and highest title of those present was the most evident. With every house party – in fact, with every occasion he happened to put on – he had always shown his guests around his manor house. Every single thing of importance was pointed out, he would hear the remarks of his guests and find himself beaming with gratification and self-satisfaction. Patrick was well aware that it did nothing but stoke his arrogance further still, but he did not care. This was just as he wished it.

Which was why it now unsettled him that he felt nothing of his usual delight. There was only that dullness which crept into his mind and lingered there, holding onto him with a vice-like grip.

Patrick grimaced.

"This is all quite wonderful, Lord Addenbrook!"

His smile did not light up his eyes.

"Thank you, Lady Foster."

"You must be in great demand whenever you go to London."

Her eyebrow lifted gently as if she were asking him a question in such a statement. Catching Lord Hogarth wiggling his eyebrows in earnest, Patrick quickly understood what the lady meant and immediately inclined his head.

"You are very kind, Lady Foster. I admit that I am often sought out by a great many of the *ton*. However, I prefer to choose my own company which is why you will find me here surrounded by those I have particularly sought out."

His smile spread across his face and Lady Foster –

much to Patrick's surprise – blushed as though she were a green girl, unused to such gentlemanly compliments.

"I quite understand, Lord Addenbrook. If you will excuse me, I must go and speak to my daughter."

Patrick nodded and watched as the lady moved away.

"If you are not careful, you will have Lady Foster's attention instead of her daughter's!"

Lord Hogarth elbowed Patrick none too gently in the ribs, making him grunt. Lord Hogarth was grinning, and Patrick found himself surprised that he was not doing so also. His eyes lingered on Lady Foster. She was a little older than himself but by no means unattractive. But it was her daughters that Patrick had thought to encourage. He had wanted to capture their interest, had wanted them to return to London so that news of his character and the house party was spread through all of London. That would encourage the *ton* to think all the better of him and might, in turn, make his house parties become renowned so almost everyone in London would wish to receive an invitation.

That did not seem to be of such importance now.

"You are not pleased by her interest?"

"Indeed, I am," Patrick protested, quickly, not wanting to give his friend any wrong impression. "It is just a trifle unexpected."

Lord Hogarth's eyes flared, and he laughed aloud.

"Good gracious! Unexpected? When your intentions were to gain such interest in the first place?" Patrick sighed and rolled his eyes, refusing to answer such a question. "You are still a little melancholy, I think." Lord Hogarth's tone suddenly became more serious. "You have not had any news of your brother?"

Sending a hard look towards his friend, Patrick hesitated, then shook his head.

"No. I have written to my brother's man of business to enquire about his debts in the hope that the reply will aid me somewhat." He shrugged, seeing Lord Hogarth's frown darken his brow. "What else can I do? I have had men out searching for him for some time and still, he evades me."

Lord Hogarth leaned in close to Patrick, his frown suddenly gone and quickly replaced with a bright grin.

"You could consider Lady Foster, could you not?"

"And how would that aid me in my search for my brother?"

"It would not! But it would distract you from your melancholy and, I am sure, bring a little more contentment to your circumstances."

He grinned and Patrick could not help but snort with laughter at the ridiculousness of such a statement.

"Might I enquire as to what such great humor is about?"

Patrick shot a hard look towards his friend as Lord Kingston ambled across the room to join them, one eyebrow lifted enquiringly. Patrick had not, as yet, managed to have any great depth of conversation with the gentleman but thus far, Lord Kingston appeared to be a pleasant fellow who made amiable conversation and was gentlemanly in all respects.

"Lord Hogarth is attempting to ridicule me, Lord Kingston," Patrick replied, seeing Lord Hogarth clap one hand to his chest in mock horror. "But I am glad to state that he is having very little success."

"I am doing no such thing," Lord Hogarth exclaimed, whilst grinning so broadly that it made it quite clear that this was exactly what he had been doing. "Now, are we to go to the library, Addenbrook? I had hoped to find a quiet corner into which to pull a certain young lady."

His voice dropped and his eye flicked in a wink which made Patrick roll his eyes.

"You are not particularly subtle but yes, we shall go to the library." Waving one hand, he gestured for Lord Hogarth to continue on. "You may lead the way."

Lord Kingston said nothing, but Patrick noticed how he watched Lord Hogarth leave. Did he think poorly of the fellow – or of him, for allowing Lord Hogarth to do as he pleased?

"You have been most kind to invite me to your house party, Lord Addenbrook."

Patrick smiled.

"But of course."

The expectation of self-satisfaction growing in his chest was not met, for nothing unfurled, nothing sent pride swirling through him.

"It has been something of a distraction from my grief," Lord Kingston continued, shaking his head to himself. "Although I should like to speak to you about the circumstances in which we both find ourselves."

Patrick nodded.

"Of course. I apologize that there has not been time as yet."

Lord Kingston waved a hand.

"But of course. I quite understand. As I have said, I have been glad of the distraction." A small, sad smile lingered as he looked all around him. "You have a most exceptional estate, Lord Addenbrook. I find myself quite in awe of it."

Again, Patrick waited for a few moments so that he might feel that bubbling sense of pride fill him but, again, it did not come.

"I thank you."

"My dear Albina would have thought this a remarkable estate also."

There was a twist of sadness in his voice and Patrick knew it would be unfair of him not to remark upon it.

"You must care for her deeply."

Lord Kingston nodded. The other guests were meandering towards the door, their heads turning this way and that so that they might look at the remaining artworks as they followed Lord Hogarth from the room.

"As I thought she cared for me."

Patrick frowned, his attention returning solely to Lord Kingston. Had the fellow meant to say such a thing? Lord Kingston was looking up at one of the portraits and appeared to be lost in thought, making Patrick uncertain as to whether or not he had meant such a remark to be overheard.

"You do not believe that she cares for you?" Unwilling to allow such a question to linger in his mind, Patrick spoke openly. "Did something take place which suggested that she did not?"

Lord Kingston blinked for a few moments, then gave a half smile.

"There was a small disagreement between us before her disappearance, but nothing of true significance. I do hope that when she discovers that I have been searching for her – regardless of what has happened to her, she will realize the true extent of my devotion."

"Quite." Patrick's frown did not lift. There was something that Lord Kingston was not telling him, something which had made Lady Albina doubt his devotion to her. Silently, Patrick wondered if that had something to do with the lady's disappearance. Mayhap her parents had removed her from London without explanation, realizing that Lord

Kingston was not the best of gentlemen as they had once believed. Gesturing towards the door, he began to walk towards it, with Lord Kingston beside him. "My brother, however, has no need to question my devotion to him."

Lord Kingston gave him a half-smile.

"I am sure that is true."

Although he has every right to question my willingness to share what is mine with others – including himself.

Patrick grimaced but did not speak such a thought aloud. Lord Kingston had no need to know of Patrick's inner struggle.

"And this is your brother here, I believe?"

Lord Kingston stopped and turned towards the wall to his left, gesturing towards the portrait of Patrick's brother.

"Yes, that is my brother, James Dutton."

"There is certainly a family resemblance!"

Patrick smiled a little sadly, wondering if he would ever be able to see or speak to his brother again.

"Indeed there is, for we both have the familial broad nose which appears to take up half of our faces!"

Both he and Lord Kingston laughed, although Patrick noticed that Lord Kingston did not immediately disagree with his statement.

"And might I enquire as to who this particular lady might be?"

Lord Kingston gestured to the portrait of a young lady and immediately, Patrick's smile fell from his face.

"That is my brother's late wife and the mother of my nephew, Henry."

"I see." Lord Kingston threw him a sympathetic glance. "She was quite lovely."

"Indeed, she was."

"And what has become of your nephew?"

Patrick hesitated. He had not wanted any of his guests to become aware of Henry's presence here, mostly in order to protect his own reputation. It made him a little lesser in the *ton*'s eyes if he had a charge to consider.

"He is being cared for by those I have appointed," he replied, somewhat mysteriously. "I–"

Out of the corner of his eye, he saw a quick movement and realized, with a sudden thump to his stomach, that his nephew was currently hiding himself behind one of the marble statues on the other side of the room. His first response was to be severely irritated with Henry and, thereafter, with Miss Trean, only to suddenly recall that he had promised her that a maid would care for the boy if she was unwell. Evidently, she was still rather poorly.

"The lady does look a good deal like Lady Albina."

Patrick forced his head to turn back towards the paintings, praying that the maid would come to find the child soon.

"Oh?"

"The fair hair that appears to run in a golden cascade down her back." Lord Kingston was speaking softly, as if directly towards the portrait itself. "And with such blue eyes that one might lose oneself in their depths."

Patrick's thoughts immediately turned to the only other young lady he knew with such blue eyes, finding his lips curving gently.

"I know precisely what it is that you speak of, Lord Kingston."

"Uncle."

The shock that went through Patrick had him pinned to the floor for a few moments. Had the child truly just approached him and decided to speak to him in such a calm voice and respectful manner? Where was the screaming child who flung himself around the room without hesitation? The child who would refuse to listen to a single word that Patrick said? Clearing his throat and seeing Lord Kingston's curious look, Patrick turned back towards the gentleman.

"It appears that we are to be joined by my nephew, Lord Kingston." Feeling rather uncomfortable at the meeting, given that he had begged for Henry to be kept away from the guests, Patrick cleared his throat before turning his attention to Henry. "Yes, Henry?" He tried to keep his voice pleasant even though he wanted to express his frustration to the boy over his insistence on interrupting them both. "Is there a reason that you are here and not with Miss Trean?"

Henry blinked up at him, his hands clasping tight in front of him, his shoulders a little hunched.

"Miss Trean is unwell. But I have lost Jean."

"Jean?" Patrick repeated, only to recall that the maid named Jean was now looking after Henry. "And might I ask if you lost her deliberately?" Henry shook his head but licked his lips, then reached up and took Patrick's hand. A jolt went straight through him. The little boy had never once shown any sort of trust in him and now, his small fingers were curling around Patrick's and the softness in his eyes showed no fear. Patrick swallowed hard. This was all Miss Trean's doing and he found himself overwhelmingly grateful towards her for it. "Henry?"

Another voice came from the door and Patrick's eyes flared in surprise. Henry had just told him that Miss Trean was unwell and now here she was, calling for him?

"Do excuse me."

Excusing himself from Lord Kingston, Patrick hurried towards the door which Henry was busy attempting to drag him towards. Miss Trean stepped out into the hallway, only for her eyes to flare as she then immediately shrank back into the shadows of the room behind her.

"Miss Trean." Patrick found himself reaching for her without having any real understanding as to why. "Pray, do not fear showing yourself to Lord Kingston. I know that I have begged you to keep Henry from the guests, but it seems that the child is eager to make the acquaintance of one of them at least!" His hand caught hers and he gave her a gentle tug forward, which she did not resist. Patrick blinked in surprise at the paleness of her cheeks. "You are not recovered, Miss Trean."

"Jean informed me that Henry had disappeared, and I came at once to search for him." Miss Trean's voice was low, practically a whisper. "I have found him now so I shall return at once to the schoolroom. I–"

"My uncle was not cross with me, Miss Trean!"

Henry's cheerful voice interrupted them both and Patrick glanced down at the child, a little surprised to hear him say such a thing. Miss Trean bent forward and patted the boy's head.

"Did I not tell you that your uncle cares for you?" she said softly, only to lift her head and look over Patrick's shoulder. Patrick watched as she pressed her lips tight together, whitening them. Her eyes were huge as if she were suddenly very afraid. "Come, Henry. Let us return upstairs where we ought to be."

Patrick's hand restrained her.

"Miss Trean." He could not seem to pull his fingers away from hers, wanting to warm her cold skin. "Are you quite all right?"

Miss Trean swallowed hard but tried to smile – a smile that Patrick did not believe.

"I am quite all right. I require a little more rest, but I shall do so in the nursery this afternoon."

Her fingers pressed his and fire erupted in Patrick's stomach at the way she responded to him. *She has not yet pulled her hand away.*

"There is nothing for you to fear," he told her gently. "I know that Lord Kingston will not mind that there is a child and a governess present. Perhaps I ought not to have spoken with such firmness before. You need not hide yourselves away entirely, Miss Trean. Not if Henry is struggling with such a thing."

"I am sure we shall be quite all right for these next three days." Miss Trean's voice was tight. "Pray excuse us, my Lord. I will make certain not to disturb you again."

Patrick could say nothing to convince her and as her hand slipped out of his, he let out a heavy sigh. Miss Trean took Henry's hand and hurried away, just as Lord Kingston's presence was felt beside Patrick.

"That was the governess, I suppose?"

Nodding, Patrick turned back to the gentleman.

"It was. Shall we make our way to the library with the others?"

Lord Kingston nodded but did not smile, a sharpness in his eyes, his lip curling slightly as one eyebrow lifted.

"You have... enjoyed her company, I presume?"

The fire that had caught Patrick's stomach at Miss Trean's touch now erupted into a raging torrent that had his hands curling into fists. It took all of his strength to speak calmly whilst, inwardly, wanting to do something a good deal more so that Lord Kingston would not think so poorly of Miss Trean.

"Miss Trean is the governess to my nephew and nothing more."

His words were clipped, his tone icy.

"But she must be quite lovely, so why should you not?" Lord Kingston laughed and Patrick's hands tightened still further. "I did not manage to take a prolonged look at her, but her figure is certainly comely even in such a drab gown. That, I should think, would be a great temptation to any gentleman."

"I am more than able to control my response to such temptations," Patrick replied, curtly. "This way, if you please."

He gestured for Lord Kingston to make his way ahead of him, struggling against the burning anger which now sent fire into every single part of him. Lord Kingston did not seem to notice Patrick's reaction and continued remarking further on Miss Trean and why he should have no qualms about using such a young lady for his own pleasures. Patrick, however, remained a little further behind the gentleman, taking in long, steadying breaths and questioning why it was that he felt such a fierce and determined anger over the gentleman's remarks. After all, it was not as though Miss Trean meant anything to him. She was only his nephew's governess and, as such, remained as one of Patrick's staff. It was preposterous to believe that he felt anything other than gratitude for what she had done for Henry.

So why was it that his heart was angry and sore, as if injured on her behalf? Why had he responded with such anger? And why had it been that his heart had quickened just a little when he had taken her hand? Unable to answer such questions, Patrick dropped his head and ran one hand over his eyes. Whatever the cause, it appeared that Miss Trean was becoming a little more to him than he had ever expected and that was a very troubling thought indeed.

CHAPTER TEN

Albina could not sleep. Every sound, every scuffle from the rats made her believe that Lord Kingston would, at any moment, suddenly appear at her door, storm inside, and demand to know what she was doing at Lord Addenbrook's home. When Jean had first come to her, Albina had been resting with a cool cloth over her eyes, struggling with the lingering headache which had hit her from the very first moment she had woken. But when Jean had told her that Henry had run from her, Albina had not had any thought for her painful head. Instead, she had risen and begun to help Jean search. The dread which had come with the realization that she would have to go downstairs to look for the boy had been almost paralyzing. The fear that she would walk directly into Lord Kingston had made her heart explode with panic, but yet the fear in Jean's eyes had been all the greater. Indeed, the maid had been almost frantic with upset, terrified that Lord Addenbrook would remove her from her position for her failure – an upset that Albina had done her best to remove from the maid's shoulders. With no other choice but to go downstairs, Albina had curled her fingers tightly into her palms, straightened her shoulders, and with ragged breathing, had quietly tiptoed down the stairs.

Her eyes closed but not from tiredness. Recalling her fear and her then bountiful relief when another maid told her where Henry had gone *and* that the guests were in the library, Albina had gone with a good deal more confidence to find him – only to walk out into the very space where Lord Kingston had been standing.

A swirl of fear forced Albina to breathe deeply, turning over onto her side as she fought back the panic that threatened to overwhelm her once more. The shock of seeing him had driven her backward, back into the shadows of the doorway whilst Henry had immediately dragged Lord Addenbrook towards her. With Lord Addenbrook standing in front of her, Albina had been able to hide from Lord Kingston but when he had begun meandering towards them all, she had practically fled from them both with Henry in tow.

She had to pray that he had not recognized her, but could not be fully convinced of it.

Another scuffle had her pulling the blankets closer around her. The rats were very busy indeed this evening and Albina squeezed her eyes closed tightly, disgust shivering down her back.

And then she heard it.

A creak.

Her eyes flew open, staring out into the darkness as she held her breath.

There it was again. Another creak, followed shortly after by another – as if someone were walking along the hallway outside her bedchamber – and outside Henry's bedchamber.

Henry.

Albina froze in place, her mind filled with thoughts of Henry. Whoever it was, she had a duty to protect Henry from them. Pushing herself up, Albina silently swung her legs down, her toes touching the cold floor. She shivered hard and reached out blindly for something, anything to wrap around herself, her fingers finding her cloak which she had left draped over the edge of her chair. Her toes dipped into her slippers, stealing away some of the cold. Fear wove itself around her limbs, tying her to her bed.

I cannot.

Albina closed her eyes and listened carefully. There *was* someone outside. She could hear the creak of the floorboards still – and realized with shock that the scuffling had stopped. Had the rats been frightened away by this person's presence?

I must make sure that Henry is safe. It is my duty.

The affection which had grown in her heart for the child forced her into action, pulling her away from the ties of fear. With a heart which began to pound furiously, Albina crossed the room on silent feet, and brought her hand to the handle of her door. Turning the handle, she winced as it squeaked gently, stilling at once for fear that whoever was outside would hear it.

But no-one came and Albina, taking in a steadying breath, pulled open the door slowly and carefully. Releasing the handle, she poked her head out – and saw a flickering light coming from along the hallway.

Whoever it was had a candle.

Quite what she would do if she did find someone lurking, Albina did not know. But the thought of leaving Henry alone and defenseless was not one she could accept and thus, she stepped out of her bedchamber and took three steps up the hallway.

The floorboards creaked under her feet and Albina caught her breath as the flickering light ahead of her suddenly shifted. It moved back towards her, and she clamped one hand over her mouth and remained just as still as she could. The light had not touched her as yet, but if it drew any closer, she would have no other choice but to return to her bedchamber and try again.

Something scraped and Albina closed her eyes, trying to push away any dark thoughts about what might occur if she was discovered. The sounds grew but she stayed where she was, waiting to see what would happen next.

But when she opened her eyes, the light was gone.

Albina blinked in the darkness, surprise filling her chest. Dropping her hand to her side, she walked towards Henry's room, aware of the creaking from the floorboards under her feet but having very little she could do about it. Her heart was beating so loudly that it was painful, but Albina did not even acknowledge it. Feeling her way along the hallway, she came to where the light had been – just outside of Henry's room.

But there was no light there now and, surely, she would have heard the door open and close if the person had gone inside. So where had this person gone? And why were they here, in the schoolroom and nursery?

You must inform me at once if such a thing should happen again.

Lord Addenbrook's words flew into Albina's mind as she opened Henry's door carefully, trying not to make a sound. Her eyes had adjusted to the dark, but she still walked closer to make certain that Henry was still asleep in his bed.

Relief flowed through her. Henry was sound asleep, for his breathing was heavy. Relieved, Albina made her way back out into the hallway and stood for a few moments, considering. Her skin prickled as fear began to push itself into her heart and mind once more. This person could be anywhere nearby, ready to strike out at her should she take even an unwitting step towards him. She would have to leave Henry and go at once to Lord Addenbrook, in the hope that he might be able to see her. It was very late but Albina knew that gentlemen such as he did not always retire early, especially when there were guests. She would have to be very careful indeed, however. Lord Kingston could not see her face.

I must harness whatever courage I can muster.

The tightness in her throat grew as she ran one hand along the wall, walking slowly towards the staircase which she knew was only a short distance ahead of her. Her breathing was quick, but her steps slow, for without a light it was very difficult indeed to see ahead of her. It was as if a thousand pins were being stuck into her skin, such was her fright, her terror that this particular person would step out of the darkness and attack her.

But then she found the staircase, and her fingers gripped tightly onto the rail as she slowly began to descend. With her thick cloak wrapped over her shoulders and her feet encased in slippers, Albina knew she must look a very strange sight indeed, but it could not be helped.

"And that is when I heard him say that...."

Albina shrank back but the two ladies were already through another doorway, their lingering conversation no longer able to be overheard. Her heart was pounding with such a fierceness that she could not seem to catch her breath. Where should she go? Where would Lord Addenbrook be?

The study.

If he was not there, then Albina would have to ring the bell and beg whatever servant came to answer the bell for their help – but it was a way for her to stay out of sight of the guests. Pulling the hood of her cloak over her fair hair, she stole down the hallway, relieved that there were only a few flickering candles with which to guide her steps. She was nothing more than a wraith, a dark shadow that faded away with all manner of swiftness. Even if she was seen, Albina was certain she would not be noticed.

Nearing Lord Addenbrook's study, Albina was about to step straight towards it when she heard Lord Kingston's voice.

"You, there!"

She turned, her hand grasping tightly at her cloak, her face still half hidden.

"If you are trying to hide your face, Lady Mary, then I must tell you there is no longer any need to do so. I have been waiting for you."

Albina swallowed then tried to speak.

"I am not Lady Mary." Her voice was high pitched, her words barely audible. "Excuse me."

"Ah, you are Miss Trean." She could see him ambling towards her, his silhouette outlined against the flickering candlelight. "Why do you not keep me company until Lady Mary arrives? I should be glad to know you a little better, since Lord Addenbrook thinks so very highly of you."

Albina shook her head.

"Excuse me. I have an urgent matter I must discuss."

Without even thinking, she cut past him, turned the

handle of the study door, and practically threw herself inside.

"Good gracious!"

Lord Addenbrook stared at her as she slammed the door closed and leaned against it, breathing heavily.

"Miss... Trean?"

"I beg your pardon, my Lord." Her breathing was so ragged that she struggled to have push the words from her lips. "Lord Kingston is...."

She could not find a way to tell him what had just occurred, but Lord Addenbrook seemed to understand for he immediately came over to the door and turned the key in the lock.

Albina could not help but let out a long sigh of relief and slipped the hood from her head, still sagging back against the door.

"Lord Kingston is waiting for someone, I presume?" Nodding, Albina closed her eyes, aware of the tears which threatened to push themselves from her eyes. She had been quite justified in her opinion of Lord Kingston. There was nothing that drew her towards him now. "Is there a reason, Miss Trean, that you have flung yourself into my study with such abandonment?" Lord Addenbrook had not moved away but stayed close to her, his eyes searching her face. "That is not to say that you are unwelcome but –"

"I am certain that there was someone upstairs, my Lord." Albina's could hear the tremble in her voice and was actually relieved when Lord Addenbrook's hand caught hers, finding strength in his presence. "I made certain that Henry was quite safe before I came to find you. I did not know what else to do."

Lord Addenbrook said nothing, his jaw tight. His eyes

searched her face and then, much to her astonishment, he leaned closer.

"Stay here." His voice was low, his breath whispering across her cheek. "Lock the door behind me for I do not think that Lord Kingston is the most... self-controlled of gentlemen."

She nodded, her throat constricting.

"Sit. Rest. I will return shortly."

Albina shivered but she nodded. Lord Addenbrook gazed into her eyes for another long moment and, much to her astonishment, brushed his fingers lightly down her cheek for just a second before he turned, dropping her hand from his grasp, and then unlocking the door.

"Miss Trean."

Hardly able to move such was the shock and the warmth that ran through her in equal measure, it took Albina all of her strength to stand away from the door. Lord Addenbrook held her gaze for one moment longer, then pulled it open and stepped outside, closing it quickly behind him. Albina's fingers slipped as she turned the key in the lock, but it was soon done, leaving her alone in Lord Addenbrook's study.

With the silence came a rush of emotion which she could not quite push aside. When the tears came to her eyes, she was unable to blink them away and thus, with a sob, Albina made her way to a chair, sank into it, and put her hands over her face. The tears ran freely but Albina allowed them to do so, overcome by all that had taken place. First, there had been her fright in hearing that person upstairs, then the dread at being discovered as she rushed to find Lord Addenbrook, and then the horror that Lord Kingston had found her.

"And then he stood near me," Albina whispered to

herself, her frame still shaking slightly as her tears began to subside. Lord Addenbrook had been so close to her, had taken her hand and had gazed into her eyes – and she had felt herself safe in his presence. When his fingers had grazed her cheek, she had barely been able to comprehend it, save for the heat that had poured into her face. Butterflies were dancing all through her and, despite her tears and her shock, a small smile was lifting her lips.

Lord Addenbrook had his faults, certainly, but the way he had gone to Henry without hesitation spoke well of his character. The obvious care and concern he had for the boy had touched her heart and, given the fact that she had the confidence simply to walk into his study and trust that he would not grow angry with her for doing so also spoke of his merits.

But am I truly allowing myself to feel something for him?

Her silent question could not be answered. Albina lifted her head completely and dropped her hands into her lap. Lord Kingston was clear in his intentions towards her – thinking her only a governess – and Albina had never been so disgusted in all of her life. Lord Addenbrook, on the other hand, had drawn near her, had touched her cheek, and held her hand but had never made any attempt to take advantage of her and, for whatever reason, Albina was aware that she trusted him not to do so. It was, she presumed, because he had only ever treated her with respect and consideration in the short time of their acquaintance as well as the fact that the staff had never said a single word to her about Lord Addenbrook's ways. She trusted him. But she knew now that she could never again trust Lord Kingston.

Her choice had been a wise one but there was no way for her to prove that to her father, not now that she had run away from home. If she returned, he would only seek to force her to wed Lord Kingston to save her from any whisper of scandal, and would not be willing to listen to a single thing she had to say. Her only choice for the present was to remain as governess.

The knock at the door startled her. It came once, twice and three times and Albina rose quickly, her heart beating furiously as she went to turn the key. Pulling it back, she stepped aside as Lord Addenbrook walked inside. He then closed the door and turned the key again before turning back towards her and grasping her hand.

"Are you quite well, Miss Trean?"

She nodded, relieved to see him again.

"You are uninjured, I hope?"

"I am quite safe." He squeezed her hand and then released it gently. "Come, sit down, Miss Trean. I have sent three footmen to go over every room carefully, although I have warned them not to wake Henry with their endeavor."

With relief, Albina took up her seat once more, looking back steadily at Lord Addenbrook. His brows were low over his eyes, and he was watching her steadily as if she held some answers to his as yet unasked questions. Albina's stomach twisted but she did not speak, wondering suddenly if Lord Kingston had, in fact, recognized her and had gone on to tell Lord Addenbrook the truth. Her fingers twined together, her palms becoming sweaty and her breathing quickening. Still, Lord Addenbrook said nothing. Albina's mouth went dry. Was he about to tell her that he knew everything?

"You are very brave, Miss Trean." Albina did not know what to say. Was he referring to her presence here in his house, pretending to be a governess? "Lord Kingston caused you additional problems and for that, I am sorry."

The tight knot in her stomach loosened and Albina let out a slow, careful breath.

"That is not your doing, my Lord."

"I told him to join this house party, even though I did not know his character. His sadness over the loss of his betrothed encouraged me to have him visit here so that he and I might share our situations and mayhap find something – although I do not know what – that might encourage one or both of us." Closing his eyes, he shook his head. "Perhaps as a balm to my guilt."

Albina tilted her head.

"You have no guilt to speak of when it comes to your brother's disappearance, I am sure."

Lord Addenbrook's eyes swirled for a moment, his lips pressed flat.

"I have no part in his disappearance, certainly, but I have a great deal of guilt in the fact that he has not returned home or to his son here – and that I have done very little in the interim."

Leaning forward in her chair, Albina spoke firmly.

"That is not so, my Lord, I am sure. You have been searching for him. You have men out still, do you not?" Seeing his nod and wishing to encourage him, Albina tried to smile. "You are doing a great deal, Lord Addenbrook."

"I should be doing more!" One hand thumped down hard on the edge of the chair, making her jump. "Instead, I am throwing house parties and attempting to push myself into amusement and joviality. I am doing what pleases *me*, rather than thinking about my brother and my nephew." Closing his eyes, he rubbed his fingers over his brow. "I am inclined towards arrogance, as you know, Miss Trean. I am eager that others should be reminded of my status and my wealth – and yet now, I find that such things no longer hold any interest for me." Albina did not know how to respond. Lord Addenbrook was informing her of things that were so very personal to him that she was uncertain as to what one ought to say. "However, at least I am not false." His jaw jutted forward. "I am not at all convinced that Lord Kingston is truly as sorrowful as he appears to be about the loss of his betrothed."

Albina's heart squeezed painfully.

"You do not believe him?"

"A gentleman who declares himself to be so fond of his betrothed but is yet willing to behave most inappropriately with the other young ladies present is no gentleman at all." His lips pulled to one side. "That does not speak well of myself, however, for I am a gentleman who has never shied away from dalliances, Miss Trean. However, should I ever find myself in such a position as Lord Kingston where I find myself fond of a particular young lady, I can assure you that I would never continue in such affairs." Embarrassed, Albina looked away only to hear Lord Addenbrook groan. When she glanced back at him, he was pinching the bridge of his nose, his eyes screwed up tight. "I should not have spoken so openly."

Albina wanted to agree, but found herself so uncomfortable that she could not form even a single word. Lord Addenbrook was being quite honest, certainly, but she was not in any sort of position where she could respond well. *Although,* she told herself, *you trust that he would keep his word and would not behave so, should he ever find himself inclined towards.... a young lady.*

Her cheeks heated and she closed her eyes. Why did she suddenly want Lord Addenbrook to be inclined towards *her*? It was ridiculous, for he believed her to be a governess and were she to reveal the truth, Albina could not be sure that he would respond with understanding. She would have broken his trust in her completely and there might be no returning to their current relationship, such as it was. At present, it was not a risk she could take, despite her strange, tumultuous feelings.

Lord Addenbrook sighed heavily and drew her attention back towards himself.

"What I am trying to say, Miss Trean, is that I made a mistake in inviting Lord Kingston here. I would beg you to be very careful indeed if you have cause to come downstairs again for fear that he may be watching for you."

Albina's throat constricted and her hands grasped the arms of the chair tightly.

"Watching for me?"

Lord Addenbrook nodded.

"He has remarked upon your presence here already and the fact that he was attempting to coerce you this very evening does not give me cause to think well of him. You must be careful, Miss Trean." Letting out a frustrated hiss between his teeth, Lord Addenbrook raked one hand through his hair, grimacing as he did so. "Would that I could think of a way to remove him from this house."

Trying to calm her frantic thoughts, Albina steadied her mind and tried to speak.

"Is there any thought as to who it was that was upstairs, my Lord?" she asked, hearing the tremor in her voice. "I fear for Henry's safety."

Lord Addenbrook shook his head.

"It is difficult to say, Miss Trean. It could be one of the guests, I suppose, but what would be their purpose in such a thing?" Spreading his hands, he shrugged. "I will have a footman walk through the schoolroom and the nursery each morning and evening in the hope of making sure of your protection."

"Thank you, Lord Addenbrook." She rose. "I will leave you now."

He was by her side before she could take even a single step away from her chair, his hand on her arm.

"I will accompany you to the staircase, Miss Trean." There was no request, no asking her permission but rather a determination that he would do so. "And again, if there is ever something that concerns you, I beg of you to come to me at once – if you are able."

Albina looked up into his face and found herself suddenly yearning to be in his embrace. She wanted to feel the strength of his arms about her so that she might rest her head on his shoulder and allow the weight she carried to dissipate for just a few moments.

But instead, she nodded, stepped to one side, and waited for him to walk to the door so that they might walk out of the study together.

CHAPTER ELEVEN

"You appear fatigued this morning, old boy." Patrick grimaced as Lord Hogarth clapped him hard on the back. "Is there a particular reason for your fatigue?"

Lord Hogarth's eyebrow lifted high, but Patrick immediately shook his head.

"If you are suggesting that I had a dalliance last evening then you are quite mistaken."

Seeing his friend's shoulders drop and his smile fade made Patrick wince inwardly. Was this all that Lord Hogarth cared about? Was this what *he* had once held up as important? The realization of that made him want to drop his head into his hands in shame, for it was as if someone was holding up a mirror to what he was truly like and he did not like the reflection staring back at him.

Ever since Miss Trean arrived, I have found myself changing. Patrick's smile was grim. *I cannot imagine that she must think particularly highly of me.*

Why that mattered to him when she was only a governess and he a Marquess, Patrick could not say, but for whatever reason, what Miss Trean thought of him was of great importance. She had been the one to make him realize that he needed to speak and act more gently around Henry. She had been the one to encourage him as regarded his search for his brother. She had been the one who had invoked such a sense of urgency and protectiveness within him that he had found himself thinking of her very often indeed. And given the way he found himself speaking – albeit a little too openly at times – she had seen more of his heart and heard more of his troubles than any other. There was something quite remarkable about the lady, and Patrick had to admit that he admired her.

And there is more to your admiration than just a grudging respect.

A flush hit his cheeks and he turned away from his friend, not wanting Lord Hogarth to see the color in his face. Miss Trean was quite lovely and there had come within him last evening such an urge to wrap her in his arms that it had taken a great deal of effort to turn away from her. He was not the sort of gentleman to take advantage of his staff and that included Miss Trean, no matter how much he found himself eager to grow close to her.

Get hold of yourself. She is your nephew's governess!

Patrick nodded to himself and picked up a piece of toast to set it on his plate. Given just how much Henry adored Miss Trean, Patrick could never do anything to ruin the situation here at the house. His nephew had been through quite enough already. A glimmer of a smile brushed across his lips as he recalled how Henry had taken his hand, his eyes trusting as he had looked up into Patrick's face. That had meant a great deal to Patrick and again, he had found himself grateful to Miss Trean for her part in it all.

"You have not listened to a single word I have said these last few minutes!"

Patrick looked up.

"I beg your pardon?"

Lord Hogarth blew out a frustrated breath.

"I said, you have not been paying even the least bit of attention to me, is that not so? Your mind is elsewhere!"

Shrugging, Patrick picked up his plate and took it to the dining table. At the moment, it was only himself and Lord Hogarth present and Patrick presumed it would be some time before the other guests rose from their slumber, given the lateness of the hour that they had all retired.

"It is."

"And what – or who – is it lingering on?"

Having no wish to discuss Miss Trean with his friend, Patrick sat back in his chair.

"My brother, of course."

The glint faded from Lord Hogarth's eyes.

"Oh. I see." The smile that had been ready and waiting now retreated back into the shadows. "I quite understand. Is there any news?"

Patrick shook his head.

"No, there is none."

"I recall that you said you intended to write to your brother's man of business."

"I have had no reply as yet," Patrick responded, reaching to pour some coffee into two china cups. "I am hopeful that I will receive a response soon, however."

Lord Hogarth frowned.

"Indeed."

"And there has been some concern that a stranger – or in fact, a guest, mayhap – has been wandering around the manor house late in the evening," Patrick continued, having no qualms about telling his friend such a thing. "I do not know who it is, but I am determined to discover them."

Blinking in surprise, it took Lord Hogarth a few moments to respond.

"Someone has been wandering around your house?"

"In the upstairs, in the nursery and schoolroom," Patrick confirmed. "I am concerned for Henry's safety and thus have made certain that the footmen now include a short search of that area in the morning, afternoon, and evening."

"Good gracious." Lord Hogarth reached for his coffee cup but did not take a sip. "That is most unsettling."

"It is." Patrick shook his head to himself, his frustration mounting that he had no idea as to who such a person might be. "Which is why, my dear friend, you find me so fatigued."

"I quite understand." Lord Hogarth leaned a little closer to him so that he might speak a tad more quietly, even though they were alone. "You say you have no idea who such a person might be?"

"I cannot even imagine why they are in the nursery and schoolroom!" Patrick exclaimed. "It is most strange."

Lord Hogarth tipped his head, then rubbed one finger across his lips before he spoke.

"Might it be something to do with your governess?"

Patrick hesitated. The idea had never come to him before now and yet, there was a measure of wisdom in the idea.

"I had not thought of that before."

"You do not know anything about her?"

A curling of his fingers told Patrick that he wanted desperately to defend the lady, even though he had no requirement to do so.

"I am sure that Miss Trean would not have come to me

in such urgency had she had any idea as to who it might have been."

"Unless she is doing so to make certain you do *not* think that she is in any way involved."

Patrick opened his mouth to state that such a notion was ridiculous, only to then close it again. He trusted Miss Trean, but Lord Hogarth was quite right to state that he did not know her very well as yet. The only reason he had hired her was on the word of his own old governess and yet, that appeared to have worked out very well thus far.

"Perhaps she does not even know that this person seeks her out and has come to you quite honestly – but it will soon become apparent to her that this man's intention is only towards her, whatever such intentions might be."

Patrick shook his head.

"She was injured the first time. Someone knocked into her."

Lord Hogarth shrugged.

"That might easily be explained. It could have been a maid or a footman who did so and now does not wish to admit to it for fear of losing their position. *Or*," he continued, seeming to relish such a discussion, "it may be that she and this... fellow became a little too amorous and she fell backward and had to, thereafter, give you *some* explanation given her dazedness."

There was no eagerness in Patrick's heart to accept such a suggestion, but no matter how hard he tried to ignore it, a little of the idea wormed its way into his mind. He could not forget it completely.

"I will consider it, but I do not think it a reasonable explanation," Patrick replied, a trifle coolly. "Now, given that this is nearing the end of our house party and that the Ball is to be tomorrow evening, let us think on much more delightful matters." He tried to smile and push all thoughts of Miss Trean away. "Who do you intend to dance with?"

Lord Hogarth grinned and immediately began to wax lyrical about who he would dance with and what he intended to do thereafter – a conversation that Patrick did not particularly enjoy. However, given that it was better than discussing the situation with Miss Trean and the strange intruder, Patrick permitted Lord Hogarth to talk for as long as he wished without interruption.

"And I presume that you have invited the various local gentry, so if my plans fail in any way, then I shall find some other young lady who might be more willing to accept my company."

"You will *not*." Patrick shook his head firmly as Lord Hogarth's bright smile faded. "You are correct that I have invited the local gentry, but the young ladies are all quite innocent and unused to such ways as yours. Thus, you will take great care not to behave inappropriately with any of them for it will not only damage their reputation but quite ruin my standing in their eyes also."

Lord Hogarth sighed heavily and rolled his eyes.

"You are always so concerned with your own situation, are you not? However, of course I shall oblige you. I must just hope that Lady Mary is as I wish her to be." His eyes danced as his smile returned. "And have you asked Miss Trean to join the evening?"

The shock of the suggestion drove straight into Patrick's heart.

"Miss Trean? No indeed, I have not."

"And why should you not? She would be quite able to mix with those of the lower classes, would she not? What is her situation?"

Patrick tried to remember.

"I believe that she is from a good family – the lower gentry, of course."

There was no particular reason why he should not offer her the opportunity to join the Ball for a short while, given that those in her class and situation would be present, but Patrick found himself reluctant to do so. It was as if he wanted to make certain that she was quite safe at all times and that, in permitting her to come to the Ball, he would not be able to do so. Anyone might speak to her, might attempt to take advantage of her – such as Lord Kingston, for that matter. His jaw jutted forward.

"Ah, you wish to keep her entirely for yourself. I see it now."

"That is not the case."

Patrick spoke harshly but Lord Hogarth only laughed.

"Well, if you do not wish to then I can have nothing to say against such a decision," he replied, holding up both hands towards Patrick. "Ah, and now here is Lord Kingston come to join us!"

Patrick's head swiveled around just as Lord Kingston closed the door behind hm.

"I bid you both good morning."

He bowed towards Patrick and to Lord Hogarth, who immediately laughed aloud and bade him to come and join them.

"I do hope that you had a restful night," Patrick murmured, a little surprised at the ball of anger which immediately ignited itself and began to roll around within him. "Lord Hogarth and I were just discussing the Ball."

"And whether or not Lord Addenbrook ought to invite the governess!" Lord Hogarth chuckled but Patrick did not miss the flicker of interest which jumped into Lord Kingston's eyes. He was quite certain that the only reason

Lord Kingston agreed was due to the fact that he was more than a little interested in garnering the governess's company – whether she wished it or not.

"I quite agree that you should, if there will be suitable acquaintances for her there," Lord Kingston stated firmly as Patrick shook his head. "Miss Fullerton would be in attendance, would she not? And she is the companion to Lady Havisham so it would be more than suitable for a governess to attend also. It would be good for Miss Trean, I am sure."

"Addenbrook does not wish to do so." Lord Hogarth held up one hand in defense as Patrick shot him a hard look. "I speak only the truth! You cannot be angry with me for that."

"Might I ask if there is any particular reason as to why you do not wish to?" Lord Kingston poured his coffee, averting his eyes from Patrick's face. "I am sure the lady would be glad of –"

"Because I do not think that a governess ought to indulge in such things," Patrick replied, firmly. It was not the truth, but it was an answer which would satisfy both gentlemen. "She has her duties, and I should not like her to be too fatigued for Henry come the morning."

Lord Hogarth grinned and Lord Kingston chuckled.

"Or mayhap it is that you wish her to be in your company only," Lord Kingston quipped as Patrick's jaw tightened. "I did see her stealing into your study last evening. And you had the audacity to inform me that you had no interest in the lady whatsoever!"

Over Lord Hogarth's screech of laughter, Patrick tried to speak.

"Miss Trean came to speak to me about a serious matter."

"In her night things?" Lord Kingston laughed, as Lord

Hogarth continued to roar with mirth. "That must have been very serious indeed."

Patrick pushed his chair back, already growing weary of the conversation *and* of both gentlemen. Frustrated, he rose and turned away, having no interest in attempting to convince them otherwise. He did not want Miss Trean's reputation to be blackened in any way, but it seemed that Lord Hogarth and Lord Kingston were determined to think of her quite poorly. Walking from the room, he found himself making his way towards the staircase which would lead to the schoolroom, suddenly determined to not only see but to speak with Miss Trean at once – although quite what he wished to say, Patrick was not yet sure.

The echoing laughter chased after him and with his jaw set, Patrick began to climb the staircase in search of the governess. The governess who would not leave his thoughts, would not remove herself from his mind and, it seemed, not from his heart either.

∽

"Miss Trean?"

Patrick walked directly into the schoolroom, only to find Miss Trean turning back from the window, her eyes wide in surprise. She had a piece of chalk in her hand, her fingers white with the dust.

"My Lord." It took her a few seconds to bob a curtsey. "Henry has just been taken by Jean to have something to eat. I allow him a short time to eat in between breaking his fast and luncheon, for it seems as though he is always a little hungry!"

She smiled but it was an uncertain one, wobbling at the corners as her blue eyes searched his. Patrick swallowed hard. Now that he had laid eyes on her, now that he was in her company, all the questions he had wanted to ask her seemed to fade from his memory.

"You – you are quite all right?"

The surprise disappeared from her eyes.

"I am quite well, my Lord. As is your nephew."

"Yes, I am aware. I had the footman inform me of Henry's situation a little earlier this morning." Closing the door, he came into the room a little more. "Miss Trean, a question has been asked of me as regards this... stranger... walking about up here, and I fear I must ask it."

She nodded and set her chalk down before picking up a cloth to wipe the dust from her fingers.

"But of course."

Patrick bit his lip. The thought of asking Miss Trean whether or not she knew the person who had been above stairs was now something of a burden, as though his mind were begging him not to ask it.

"It has been suggested to me that you might be aware of this... stranger walking about here." He saw her blink but continued on, ignoring the harsh warning in his mind. "Perhaps you have come to speak to me about him in the hope that I will never make the connection between yourself and such a person."

Miss Trean took a step back, her face paling.

"You mean to state that you believe me to be lying to you?"

Spreading his hands, Patrick tried to smile.

"It is only a question, Miss Trean and one that I think only fair to ask."

He was surprised how sharply she turned away from him. Silence grew between them, the air growing thick. *That was not a wise thing to ask her.* His mind screamed at him for his foolishness, but Patrick could not do anything now but wait for her answer.

"I should *never* do such a thing, my Lord." The tremor in her voice made Patrick close his eyes in frustration. He had ignored his conscience, had fought against the warning in his mind, and had spoken something that had caused the lady great distress. "I came to you because I was afraid. Afraid for Henry's safety, not for my own." She turned back to face him, her face white and pinched and her eyes glassy. "I would never show such disrespect, Lord Addenbrook, either *or* to myself."

It took him a moment to grasp what she meant but it soon became clear. Her character was one of uprightness and she clearly found even the suggestion of a dalliance to be completely distasteful.

"I ought not to have asked."

Miss Trean lifted her chin but despite her clear determination to hold herself together, a single tear trickled down her cheek.

"I assure you, Lord Addenbrook, I would never behave in such a way. I think too highly of both yourself and the position you have given me to *ever* do such a thing. I have been very afraid indeed to hear these footsteps. I was *injured* the first time! Did you not recall that?"

"I did." The suggestion that Lord Hogarth had made over her injury now seemed utterly preposterous and Patrick dropped his head in shame. "Forgive me, Miss Trean. I ought never to have asked you such a thing." Again, came the silence and when Patrick lifted his head, he saw Miss Trean's tear-filled eyes looking back at him. His heart ripped. He had behaved more than a little foolishly and even though she was his nephew's governess, his hired help, the pain he had caused her brought Patrick a great deal of regret. "Miss Trean, I am sorry."

She closed her eyes, and another tear ran down her cheek.

"You have every right to ask, my Lord." Her words were hard, her voice shaking. "I pray that you do not ever have cause to doubt my loyalty and consideration towards you again."

When she opened her eyes, Patrick's heart burst into flame. He swallowed against the tightness in his throat, but it only constricted all the more. The urge to pull himself close to her grew steadily and even though his mind protested that she was only a governess and that he ought not to have any such feelings for her, Patrick could not rid himself of such a desire. He would not take advantage of her. To do so would be entirely disrespectful and unfair.

Miss Trean took a small step forward, then blinked in surprise, as if astonished that she had acted in such a way.

A burst of hope flared in his chest. *If she feels anything for me, then –*

It did not make sense. He should not even be considering this, given her status and his own, but suddenly, that did not seem to matter one iota. Patrick did not know who moved first, for one moment they were apart and the very next, his arms were about her and her head was resting on his shoulder.

An explosion of fire ripped through his chest.

What are you doing?

A swell of horror and fright and wonder and delight wrapped itself all around him, seeming to tie him to Miss Trean. He could hear her breathing, the sensation of her fingers next to his collar making the floor seem to shake beneath his feet.

Patrick swallowed hard.

"Miss Trean. I do not wish to take advantage of you."

Her head lifted and she looked into his eyes. There was no longer any hint of tears.

"I do not wish to lose my position, Lord Addenbrook." Her voice was small but soft. "And yet I find that...."

She closed her eyes, and her lips moved but no words came out.

"I understand."

Patrick was all too aware that whilst he did not wish to compromise nor ruin the lady, the urge to be close to her, to have her in his arms was too strong to be ignored. What he would do next, however, required a good deal more thought.

I could propose.

Patrick waited for the shock to run through him, for ice to cloud his lungs and to push that thought far from him which, in turn, would push Miss Trean away, but it did not come. Instead, a gentle warmth seemed to brush across his cheek and through his hair like a soft summer breeze, swelling his heart gently.

"I should–" Miss Trean stepped back, her hands falling away from his chest. "Forgive me, Lord Addenbrook."

"There is nothing to forgive." Clearing his throat simply to give himself a little more time to regain his composure, Patrick tried to smile. "It is I who ought to beg for your forgiveness for ever suggesting such a thing as that. Lord Hogarth made some ridiculous assertions, and I ought not to have listened to him."

Miss Trean gave him a small, slightly wobbly smile.

"It is forgotten. I am grateful for your trust in me. I pray that you will always remember that I have thought only of Henry's safety through this matter. That my respect for you comes from the fact that I have witnessed your change towards Henry and in seeing your concern and regard for him – and for myself."

A little confused as to why she was making such a statement, Patrick merely put one hand to his heart and inclined his head gently.

"But of course."

Pressing her lips tight together, Miss Trean took a quick step towards him and put one hand out towards his chest.

"Lord Addenbrook, there is something that I –"

Just before her fingers grazed his shirt, a tap came at the door and, in an instant, Miss Trean stepped back.

"Come."

Frustrated, Patrick could not keep the bark from his voice.

"My Lord, there is an urgent matter that requires your attention." The butler's voice was a little tight, telling Patrick silently that there was true urgency to this. "It concerns your brother."

In an instant, all frustration fled.

"I beg your pardon?" He swung towards the butler, who nodded. "Speak! Tell me at once what has happened."

The butler threw a glance towards Miss Trean but did not hesitate.

"A fellow arrived from the local inn. He has begged to see you, but I did not think it suitable...." Seeing Patrick's frown, the butler paused and then dove directly into the heart of the matter. "There was a fellow sent from London with a message from your brother's man of business, my Lord. This man has only recently been discovered, but ten miles from the estate."

Patrick's stomach twisted.

"Discovered?"

The butler nodded, twisting his hands together in front of him.

"The man was badly beaten and appeared to be close to death. However, he has spent the last two days recovering at the inn and today was well enough to tell the innkeeper what had taken place."

Nodding slowly, Patrick began to understand the situation.

"And the message this man was meant to be delivering to me?"

"Quite gone," the butler replied quickly. "Everything else that this man had – including a bag of coins – was left upon him. But this letter for you was the only thing taken."

"Good gracious." Miss Trean's exclamation echoed all that Patrick felt. "So that is to say that–"

"That someone does not wish this message to reach me," Patrick muttered, darkly. "And that they will do anything to make certain I do not receive it."

CHAPTER TWELVE

"My father will come to wish me good night, I am sure of it."

The ache that came into Albina's heart whenever Henry spoke of his absent father grew with such force that it took her a moment to respond. She could not imagine what it must be like for such a small child to have lost first his mother and now, his father.

"You have a very strong hope, Henry. That is a good thing."

She smiled as the small boy sat down on the rug beside her, the sunshine sending shades of red through his otherwise brown hair.

"It is not hope, Miss Trean. I know he will come."

Albina tilted her head, studying him. The boy was smiling to himself, as if he held some great secret in his heart that she was not yet able to share.

"And then, when he does come, what shall he do?"

Perhaps it is best for him if I simply pretend along with him. That will be better than telling him the truth outright.

"Well." Henry grinned up at her, his eyes alive with

light and hope. "He will stand at the door and whisper, but I shall tell him that no one else is in my bedchamber but me! And then he will come in and sit down at the edge of my bed and I will tell him everything that I have done and that I have been learning my letters. And then he will smile and tell me that he thinks I am the most marvelous boy, and he will give me a kiss and promise to come again tomorrow."

What an extraordinary imagination.

"That sounds quite lovely."

"Oh, but I am not meant to tell you." His smile flickered and gave way to a frown. "I forgot that I am not supposed to tell you that he is coming."

Albina blinked. Suddenly this no longer sounded like a faint hope that the child was clinging on to but rather instead, it appeared to be the truth. As though Henry *was*, in fact, seeing his father.

That could not be so.

"Not supposed to tell me?"

"He will be cross with me if he finds out that I have told you." Henry was looking up at her now with wide eyes, beginning to blink rapidly. "You will not tell anyone, Miss Trean?"

Not quite certain what to make of this, Albina ruffled Henry's hair and gave him a warm smile.

"But of course, I shall not," she promised, even though her mind whirred furiously in an attempt to understand what it was that Henry truly meant. "You need not be worried."

The tears quickly faded from Henry's eyes.

"Might I go to the pond again?"

"Only for a few minutes. The guests will be returning from their carriage ride very soon and we will need to go indoors."

Pushing herself up to standing, Albina waited until Henry had removed himself from the rug before she began to roll it up. After the news from earlier this morning, Lord Addenbrook had been distracted and confused but she had been unable to offer any other advice. Lord Addenbrook had informed her that the guests were to take a short carriage ride through some of his estate and the surrounding areas which, he hoped, would allow him the opportunity to go to see this injured fellow at the inn. Albina hoped that he would be able to garner something of importance from him, for the situation was all very odd.

She bit her lip. There was a great relief in her heart that come tomorrow, it would be the final day of the house party. There was to be a grand Ball in the evening and the following morning, the guests would take their leave and be gone from the house. Then she and Henry might resume their lives as they had been before. Albina smiled to herself, looking out at the small boy as he threw some stones into the pond. She had come to care for Henry very much indeed and whilst her situation was difficult at times, Albina was grateful for her time with him.

And with the Marquess.

Closing her eyes, Albina let out a small sigh, her shoulders dropping.

"I am being ridiculous," she murmured to herself, opening her eyes again. She should not be feeling anything at all for the Marquess, but her heart did not want to let him go. The way he had pulled her into his arms had brought such a rush of feeling that she had silently begged for him to kiss her and had been disappointed when he had not. But then sense had taken hold and she had stepped back, reminding herself inwardly that she was a governess and nothing more. Albina bit her lip. The trust she had in Lord

Addenbrook was firm and secure. She believed that he would never take advantage of her and, even in their embrace, had proven such a thing by refusing to drop his lips to hers. She had seen the confusion and the struggle in his expression, his eyes slightly narrowed, his brows low and his eyes searching hers. And she had almost told him the truth.

"For if I told him I was Lady Albina then there would be no cause for him to pull back from me."

Shaking her head to herself at just how ridiculous a thought that had been, Albina called to Henry and together they began to make their way up to the house. Smiling, she ruffled Henry's hair gently. If she told Lord Addenbrook the truth, then she would lose everything. Her position here would be gone. Lord Addenbrook would no longer be able to trust her and could easily send her away. And what would she then return to? Her father's estate where, no doubt, he would seek to push her into matrimony with Lord Kingston who, evidently, was still eager to marry her. Albina scowled. No doubt Lord Kingston wished to marry her to give himself the appearance of a respectable gentleman whilst using their marriage to hide his weaknesses and selfish endeavors from the *ton*. Besides which, Albina knew all too well that she had a most excessive dowry. Perhaps Lord Kingston was in need of a great deal of coin, but she was not about to allow herself to be used that way.

"You will not tell my uncle, Miss Trean?"

Albina blinked, taking a moment to realize what Henry was saying.

"I will not tell your uncle about your father coming to see you?" she asked, as Henry nodded. "Why? Has your father asked that your uncle not know?"

Henry nodded.

"It is all a very great secret, but I forgot that I was not to tell you." Again, his chin began to wobble. "He will be upset with me."

Taking in a deep breath, Albina bent down, her skirts billowing outwards.

"My dear Henry, you must not be afraid." She did not make any promise not to tell Lord Addenbrook but attempted to reassure the child regardless. "I will do what is best for you. I care about you a great deal, so you need not worry any longer."

Henry's chin continued to wobble but he nodded, turned, and then took her hand.

"May I have sausages and eggs for breakfast?"

Albina laughed.

"You have already had breakfast!" she exclaimed, before following him into the house.

∽

Albina smiled softly and ran her hand lightly through Henry's soft hair.

"It is time for you to sleep now."

Henry frowned, shifting slightly as he lay in his bed.

"But you must go, Miss Trean."

"Go?"

"My father will not come if you stay here."

Albina hesitated, then leaned forward to kiss Henry lightly on the cheek.

"Very well."

It was as if the child had known that her intention had been to remain in the nursery to see whether or not James Dutton would appear. She had not spoken to anyone else about what the child had said, but Albina was beginning to believe that it was all quite true. However, the only way she would be able to prove it, and certainly the only way that would allow her to speak to Lord Addenbrook about what Henry had said, was if she found out for herself whether or not James Dutton was present in the house. After the news Lord Addenbrook had received yesterday about the messenger sent from London, Albina did not want to burden him with something more which could then easily turn out to be nothing more than a small child's imaginings. Leaving the room, she closed the door gently and then stood by it, thinking hard. She could wait somewhere nearby in the hope that James Dutton would appear, or she could retire to her room as she usually did – and as he would expect – before stepping out in search of him every few minutes.

Choosing the latter, Albina made her way into her bedchamber and shut the door. Rather than begin to sort out her things or make preparation for Henry's schoolwork as she usually did, Albina simply made her way to her bed and sat down. The bed creaked loudly but she did not mind. It would simply be an indication to Mr. Dutton – if he *was* present – that she was safely in her bedchamber.

Within a few minutes, she heard the familiar scuffling of the rats. Grimacing, she lifted her feet up onto the bed, her single, meager candle flickering on the small dressing table near to her bed. Closing her eyes, Albina drew in a steadying breath, imagining what would occur should she find James Dutton present in Henry's bedchamber. She did not think that he would harm her, certainly, but there would have to be some discussion.

Am I mad? Her eyes flew open. *Is this something I ought to be seeking out alone? What if there is a nefarious purpose behind his disappearance?* Tightness balled in her throat. *Perhaps this is unwise.*

She lifted her chin. No, she *had* to know for certain whether or not James Dutton was truly visiting his son each evening before she spoke to Lord Addenbrook. She could only pray that Mr. Dutton would not be angry with her and that there would be no painful consequences to her prying.

Another scuffling sound and Albina shivered furiously, tucking her feet under her skirts. It would soon be time for her to make her way into the corridor in search of this mysterious Mr. Dutton and she would have to brave the rats and the mice that were, no doubt, now scurrying around all over the floor. The thought of them brushing against her ankles lodged a silent scream in her throat but, nevertheless, Albina gathered her courage and set her feet down.

Something creaked and Albina caught her breath. If she had not been listening for it, Albina was certain she would have simply ignored such a small sound but for her now, it was very significant indeed. Holding her breath, Albina listened hard – and heard it again.

Someone is outside.

Albina moved quickly. Hurrying across the floor, she pulled open the door and stepped out into the hallway – just as a figure turned towards her.

"Dutton?"

Her voice was a breathless whisper, her heart pounding furiously against her chest.

"And this is where you hide!"

In an instant, Albina realized she had made a dreadful mistake. This was not Mr. Dutton. Lord Kingston had come in search of her, it seemed and, in revealing herself, she had practically offered herself up on a plate.

"Lord Addenbrook might not wish to take hold of you

but I, Miss Trean, am not a man who will allow such beauty to pass me by. I have not seen your face fully, I confess, but your figure is quite unmistakable." He laughed and Albina began to back away, her mind searching for something – anything she could do – that would allow her an escape. If she went into her bedchamber, he could easily push open the door for her strength would be no match for him and she did not have a key. "Come, Miss Trean! You will not refuse me, I hope?"

The slight slurring to his words made Albina realize that Lord Kingston was in his cups. With her heart screaming at her to run, to escape, Albina turned and bolted for the stairs.

Lord Kingston's footsteps clattered behind her.

"Miss Trean!" His voice was hard now, reaching out towards her as her hand found the rail of the staircase. "Do not run. I only wish to talk with you."

She was at the staircase. Having no idea what the guests were doing at present nor where they might be, Albina made for the only safe place that she could think of.

Lord Addenbrook's study.

Lord Kingston's footsteps were behind her but when she glanced back, Albina was relieved to see him staggering slightly, held back by the effects of the brandy or whisky he had imbibed earlier. She had the advantage. All she had to do was reach Lord Addenbrook's study and lock the door behind her.

It was there. She could see it. Hurrying towards it, she had one hand on the doorknob, when her arm was caught and yanked backwards.

"Miss Trean!"

Lord Kingston's voice was filled with anger, his fingers clamping down hard on her arm. Albina kept her head turned away and let out a scream as he tried to yank her back towards him. She could not allow him to see her face. Even though there were only a few candles in the hallway, Albina was sure it would be enough light for him to recognize her. But if she did not get away, then all would be lost.

Lord Kingston could take advantage of her and then she would have no choice but to marry him.

"Unhand me!"

Trying to pull her arm free, Albina twisted one way and then the next, turning this way and that in an attempt to remove Lord Kingston's hand from her arm. She heard his growl of frustration, felt his other hand brushing her shoulder and fear kicked into her stomach all the harder. With an exclamation of fear, she flung herself backward and slammed herself deliberately into Lord Kingston. The shock was enough to have him drop his hand, his breath wheezing out of him and allowing her just enough time to tug herself free of him. The sound of stitches tearing only added to her fright, her fingers slipping on the doorknob as she prayed silently that Lord Addenbrook had not locked it.

Mercifully, it opened, and Albina stepped inside, slamming it shut behind her. Lord Kingston slammed his hands hard against it, but Albina had already turned the key. She was shaking furiously, her hand going to her arm where Lord Kingston had grabbed it. Her gown was ripped and torn, cool air brushing at her exposed skin. Shuddering, Albina slipped to the floor and wrapped her arms around her knees. Even if Lord Kingston continued to pound furiously on the door, continued to shout and demand that she open it for him, Albina was certain that, for the moment at least, she was quite safe. Her mind was filled with thoughts of Lord Addenbrook, her eyes screwed up tight as she rested her head on her knees.

Please find me soon.

~

"Whatever is the meaning of this?"

"Your little governess attacked me!"

Albina swallowed hard, aware that she was still shaking dreadfully. She did not know how long she had been hiding in here, waiting for Lord Addenbrook to return, but it had felt like an age. Weary and riddled with shock, she found it difficult to lift her head.

"She attacked you?" Lord Addenbrook did not sound as though he believed Lord Kingston. "And why would she do such a thing?"

There came a garbled sound from Lord Kingston and Albina dropped her head back onto her knees. Evidently, Lord Kingston had been unable to come up with a reasonable explanation.

"And you have been standing here, thumping furiously at my door in the hope that she will hear you and allow you entry? Or is that she has shut this door upon you, and you have been doing all you can to force yourself inside?" There was a hint of double meaning in his words and Albina shuddered, revulsion writhing within her. "Prepare your things, Lord Kingston. You are no longer welcome in my home."

Albina blinked, astonishment rippling through her. Lord Addenbrook was sending Lord Kingston away? No doubt he would tell everyone he could think of what had happened and would make certain to blame Lord Addenbrook. He could make certain that Lord Addenbrook was thought of very unfavorably by society and Albina was quite certain that this was precisely what Lord Kingston would do.

"Miss Trean?"

Somehow, Albina managed to push herself to her feet. With legs that did not seem to have enough strength to hold her upright, she walked to the door and unlocked it.

Lord Addenbrook was beside in her an instant. His hands went to her arms, and she shivered, his fingers on her bare skin where her gown had ripped. When she looked up into his face, his eyes were blazing with anger.

"Lord Kingston."

It was not a question but still, Albina nodded.

"He came in search of me. He came up to my bedchamber."

"I am truly sorry, Miss Trean." Shrugging out of his jacket, he quickly wrapped it around her shoulders, covering her bare arm. "I have sent Lord Kingston away."

Gently, he led her towards a chair and helped her to sit down in it before he stood a little way back from her. Albina saw the way his hands curled tight, aware of the tightness in his frame.

"He will attempt to ruin your good name." Her voice wobbled but she lifted her chin, fearing that he would be injured by Lord Kingston's malice. "You have told me yourself that you wish for all of society to think well of you." Crossing her hands, she pulled his jacket a little more closely around her, appreciating the warmth. "It will not be so if Lord Kingston returns to London and informs the *ton* of what has occurred. He will speak naught but lies about you and then all that you have worked so hard to achieve will be broken in an instant."

"Then let him do so." Albina blinked in surprise. "Do you really think that I could simply allow him to treat you with such disrespect and continue on as my guest?" Lord Addenbrook drew closer to her but then bent down so that he was looking up into her face rather than towering over her. "Let him say what he wishes. I will refute it all. I will have those from the house party who will give their consideration of the situation and thus, the damage will be limited." His eyes were soft, and Albina's heart quickened. "Miss Trean, you must know that there are feelings I am battling with at present. Given what we have shared, it cannot come as a surprise to you. But I will never permit myself to overstep. It would not be right. Lord Kingston may not behave as a gentleman ought, but I must hope that I can attempt to do right against his wrong."

Albina swallowed.

"Not even if I return such feelings?"

Lord Addenbrook bowed his head as if battling within himself. A quiet groan reached her ears as she waited for her answer.

"It is not as simple as that. To take any action would be to ruin you."

There was no mention of matrimony and Albina's heart sank. In her position as governess, she could never even hope for such a thing. That had been a foolish thought.

But if I tell him the truth....

He spoke again, his voice soft and agonized.

"You mean so very much to Henry and have become dear to me also," he continued, unaware of her current thoughts. "But I cannot injure him and thus my feelings must remain where they are at present – hidden within my heart." His lips twisted. "There is a situation where I might consider...." Shaking his head, he took in a deep breath. "At present, with my brother absent and my nephew residing with me, I must think only of them."

The sudden ache in Albina's heart forced the truth to her lips.

"There is something I must tell you." Taking in a deep breath and aware that she was still shaking slightly, Albina reached out and set her hand gently on his shoulder. "You have trusted me, and I must now tell you that I have, from the start, broken that trust. Not because I wished to, but because I had no choice." Seeing the way his eyes flared, Albina closed hers, unable to see his face as she told him the truth. "My name is not Miss Trean." Lord Addenbrook's swift intake of breath forced her eyes open. "I am Lady Albina Waterford." Her heart was in her throat as she continued to tell him the truth. "My father wished to force me into matrimony with none other than Lord Kingston."

His eyes searched her face, wide with shock.

"You are his missing betrothed."

"I did not ever consent to wed him," Albina told him, speaking quickly as heat ran straight through her, followed by an icy cold that made her shiver. "An incident occurred which made me think very little of his character, but my father was most insistent. I could not bear the thought of being wife to a gentleman whom I despised – and who cared very little for me."

Lord Addenbrook closed his eyes.

"And so, you sought another way out."

"I could not remain there! Not when I would be pressed to marry Lord Kingston. My old governess, Mrs. Stanley, came to my aid. I have done everything I can to be as good a governess to Henry as possible. I have found myself coming to care for him a great deal – and for you." Her throat constricted but she forced herself to continue. "When Lord Kingston appeared at your house party, I was terribly afraid. It was a great relief when you asked me to make certain that both myself and Henry stayed away from the guests. I have been terrified that he would recognize me but even now, even after this... incident, it seems that he does not." Lord Addenbrook did not move or speak. His eyes remained closed, but his hand still held hers. He did not pull it away, and she felt his fingers tighten briefly. "I know that I have not been honest with you in this," Albina whispered, her stomach flooding with butterflies. "But I swear to you that I have always told you the truth in everything else."

A long, drawn-out sigh came through Lord Addenbrook's lips.

"I cannot blame you for wanting to remove yourself from Lord Kingston." His eyes opened but his jaw jutted forward as he spoke to her. "He is a selfish, cruel, and ill-intentioned fellow who has no real regard for you, despite his words to the contrary."

"Please," Albina begged, suddenly afraid that Lord Addenbrook might wish to tell Lord Kingston the truth. "Please, do not tell him that I am here."

Lord Addenbrook's eyes flared wide.

"I would not do such a thing! But this does change the situation significantly."

Albina searched his face but could not see what he was thinking.

Perhaps matrimony has never been in his thoughts. Mayhap I have been much too hopeful, much too foolish to think that he might consider marrying me. Her heart dropped low. *Then my only hope is to remain as governess.*

Her hand slid down his shoulder and to where his hand rested on the arm of the chair.

"Lord Addenbrook, if I can remain here as governess, I would be most contented. I am happy here. I love Henry dearly and I love –" She closed her eyes, her words stuttering. "I love my position here. It is not exactly what I am used to, but I have become so very happy that I cannot think of what I should do if you turn me away."

Shaking his head, Lord Addenbrook ran his hand over his eyes.

"Miss Trean – that is, Lady Albina, I do not know what I ought to do." The deep browns and greens in his eyes swirled as he gazed back into her eyes. "If I send you away, will you return to your parents?"

Albina shook her head.

"I will go to Mrs. Stanley," she told him, knowing full well that she might, one day, have to return to her parents regardless, for if she could not find another position then she would have no other choice but to do so. "If I return to them now, given my absence, the only thing that my father will seek to do is to have me wed Lord Kingston as soon as possible."

"Do you think Lord Kingston will still wish to wed you?"

Albina smiled sadly.

"I am certain of it. I have realized that he is more than a little determined to gain whatever it is he wishes and that to be refused something which he expects to be granted will infuriate him severely. Besides which, I do not think that the entirety of the *ton* believe him to be as faultless as he presents himself to be. He wants a wife so that he can appear respectable whilst continuing on just as he pleases." She spread her hands. "In addition, my father has promised the most excessive dowry to whichever gentleman weds me, and it may be that Lord Kingston has need of such coin. But I *cannot* be his wife."

"I would never force you into that position, Lady Albina." Lord Addenbrook pulled his hand gently from hers. "I cannot say what I will do at present, but I will consider everything carefully."

Albina closed her eyes, hiding her tears from him.

"Until then, you will continue with Henry. The house party is ending tomorrow with the grand Ball and, thereafter, I will think about what we will do."

Albina started as something touched her cheek and when she opened her eyes, she saw Lord Addenbrook's eyes gazing straight into hers, his hand still at her cheek.

"I am sorry I did not tell you the truth."

He gave her a small smile.

"I understand why you did not. Now that I am acquainted with Lord Kingston, I can *fully* understand your reasons." His eyes moved to her shoulders, to his jacket which covered her bare arm. "I do not care about what he will say of me, Lady Albina. It will be refuted. Regardless, that gentleman is no gentleman at all, and I do not want him in my house any longer."

Albina could not help but lean into his hand. She longed for him to hold her, grew desperate for his arms to go about her, but he did not move forward.

"Did you find out any more from the injured messenger?"

Lord Addenbrook shook his head.

"He was still much too unwell to speak. But when he recovers more, I shall return to him." Sighing, he pulled his hand away. "And you should make your way back to your bedchamber, Lady Albina."

"Miss Trean," she reminded him, a sad smile pulling gently at her lips. "For the moment, I am Miss Trean."

Nodding, Lord Addenbrook rose to his feet and then held out one hand towards her. Taking it, Albina allowed him to tug her upwards, finding her legs still a little weak and wobbly but feeling a good deal better than before. "I thank you."

"I will personally see that Lord Kingston has taken his leave," he told her, his hand still warm on hers. "You have nothing to fear now."

Albina smiled but lowered her gaze. She could not look at him for long, not when her heart was aching for him so.

"Thank you, Lord Addenbrook."

She wanted to say more but found she could not. But when he lifted her hand to his lips and brushed a kiss across the back of her hand, Albina's heart burst into life, sending fire raging through her. For a moment, it seemed as though Lord Addenbrook would catch her up in his arms, just as she hoped, but then he released her hand and stepped to one side, clearing his throat gruffly as he did so.

The moment was gone, and all Albina could do now was wait to see what Lord Addenbrook would decide to do with her – and what could so easily be either built up or broken between them.

CHAPTER THIRTEEN

*P*atrick had assumed that by the time the Ball came around, he would no longer be as shocked nor as stunned by what Miss Trean – that is, Lady Albina – had told him. However, even though his guests had high expectations of him for the evening, the only thing Patrick wanted to do was think. The music, the chatter, the laughter, and the gaiety did nothing but frustrate him and the clear expectations from his guests that he would dance with each of the eligible young ladies was greatly irritating.

She is a lady.

That thought would not leave him. It went around and around in his mind. If she was a lady of quality, then there could be nothing holding him back. There was no reason for him to pull back from his feelings for her. And yet, something was tugging him away from such an idea. Patrick could not quite place it, but there was still a part of him which remained quite uncertain. He closed his eyes.

There would be a scandal. Whether they wished it or not, somehow, someone would realize that Lady Albina had once been his governess and all of London, if not all of

England, would be abuzz with the news. Patrick's stomach twisted. That would bring him the sort of attention that he had always attempted to avoid. The high opinion that the *ton* held of him would shatter into a million pieces that could never again be restored. Was that something he was willing to give up entirely? Yes, he cared for the lady, but the thought of falling so far from grace was a difficult idea to swallow.

"Whatever is the matter with you?" Lord Hogarth sidled up to Patrick, his brow furrowed. "You appear to be in the depths of sorrow given the expression on your face!"

Patrick sighed.

"I have many things on my mind, Hogarth."

"None should be as important as the final evening of your house party, not if you wish to leave a strong impression upon your guests."

"A strong impression?"

Lord Hogarth shrugged.

"As you told me yourself, your sole intention for the house party was to show your wealth and your situation to your guests. They will, of course, think well of you and, upon their return – whether to London or to their own estate – will spread news of your marvelous house party to others. Thus, you will find yourself held in high esteem by all of the *ton*, just as you wish to be, whilst those who are inferior to you will feel themselves to be so."

There was no malice in his tone and Patrick dropped his head in embarrassment, ashamed that even only a few days ago, he had expressed that exact opinion to his friend. Had he truly been so arrogant? He had Lady Albina to thank for his change in behavior and viewpoint. In these last few days, he had found his priorities shifting so that he now considered Henry more than he considered himself.

Lady Albina – when he had known her as Miss Trean – had given him more to think about than any other. His friends appeared to be quite contented to allow him to continue on just as he was, but Miss Trean had been the one to point out his failures. She had done so without any real gentleness, but he had come to appreciate that – especially when Henry had taken his hand and so sweetly called him 'Uncle'. Even now, he could remember the gentle summer breeze on his cheek as he had stared in astonishment at her as she had told him quite frankly that his attitude towards his nephew was not at all pleasing. She had taken on none of his suggestions and Patrick was now grateful for her disregard. Henry had flourished and he had learned to see what was the most important in his life... and it certainly was not his standing in society.

Am I really willing to push her away simply to make sure that society continues to regard me more highly than almost any other?

"I do not find myself particularly concerned in that regard any longer."

His voice dropped low as stabs of guilt began to throw their way into his heart.

"No?" Lord Hogarth's eyebrows practically reached into his hair. "Indeed. That is most extraordinary."

"Perhaps it is something which I ought to have rid myself of, a long time ago," came Patrick's quick response.

Hearing Lord Hogarth speak had shown Patrick the truth of his character, as it had been before Miss Trean arriving, and he knew now that it was not a place or a person he wanted to return to. To put his own standing in society before anything else was not only ridiculous, but it was also utterly selfish. Lady Albina had given up everything to avoid marriage to Lord Kingston, risking losing her reputation in doing so, whilst he had been doing all he could to make certain that he kept his reputation pristine. That had been his priority, his *only* concern. But now, in the light of what he had learned and come to love about Lady Albina, that no longer seemed to have any of its previous significance. So why was he still trying to cling onto it?

"It is your brother; I am certain of it." Lord Hogarth spoke with confidence, dragging Patrick's attention back towards him. "You are troubled by his absence, are you not?"

"I am, of course."

"But I am certain that you will receive news from your brother's man of business very soon," came the reply, reminding Patrick that he had spoken of this particular thing to Lord Hogarth previously. "That is bound to bring you some relief."

Patrick shook his head.

"I am not certain that will occur." Quickly, he told Lord Hogarth what had taken place. "It appears that my response has been lost."

"That is dreadful." Lord Hogarth shook his head. "Will you write again?"

"No." Patrick drew in a deep breath. "As soon as is possible, I shall make my way to London and speak to my brother's man of business myself. That is the only way I shall be sure of a response." Something shifted in Lord Hogarth's expression, but Patrick could not make it out. Lord Hogarth's eyes pulled away, his mouth twisting as if frustrated. "You cannot think poorly of me for doing so."

"No, but you may think very poorly of me for being so selfish," Lord Hogarth declared, as the music began again for yet another dance. "You had spoken of having another three house parties before the Season's end and I had expected an invitation to all of them!"

Patrick shook his head.

"Alas, such things are no longer of any importance to me."

Lord Hogarth let out a long, slow breath.

"I am being quite selfish, I know. I should be thinking of your brother and your present difficulties."

Taking in another breath, Patrick decided to speak honestly to his friend.

"I am also considering matrimony," he declared, sending Lord Hogarth's eyebrows shooting towards his hairline. "Do not ask me about who it is I am considering for I will not tell you – but if I can make certain of a few things, then I fully intend to make certain that the lady I am thinking of will be my bride. And then what need have I for such things as house parties?"

His heart suddenly soared, and he drew in a long breath, his chest expanding as a broad smile spread across his face. He had made his decision. In telling Lord Hogarth that he was considering matrimony, he had chosen to push away his fears and was now truly considering proposing to the lady. Yes, there would be a scandal at some point and yes, a good deal of rumor and whispers would follow them both, but what did that matter? His happiness would come from being with the beautiful, kind, and extraordinary Lady Albina rather than from what society thought of him. From the moment he had stepped into the ballroom, his thoughts had been fixed on Lady Albina, even though he was currently surrounded by young ladies of incredible beauty. It would be difficult indeed to find a way to marry her which would bring contentment to her parents and there might be a good deal of trouble which would come from their marriage, but Patrick did not give that much consideration. The only thing he considered now was the joy which would be theirs if he could make her his bride.

It was a very freeing thought and he grinned at Lord Hogarth's response. His friend's mouth opened and closed like a fish, and he was clearly stunned, but Patrick only chuckled.

"I have astonished you, I can tell." Patrick slapped his friend on the shoulder. "You will attend the wedding, I hope?"

"You – you have already asked the lady in question?"

"I have not, but I shall do so very soon." The thought of asking Lady Albina to marry him sent his heart soaring, free of the fear and concern which had held him back only a few minutes ago. "I have every expectation that she will accept me."

Lord Hogarth shook his head.

"Good gracious." His voice was barely loud enough for Patrick to hear, particularly over the hubbub of the Ball. "Wed? Are you quite certain?"

Patrick nodded.

"More than certain, my friend." Seeing Lord Hogarth shake his head, Patrick laughed again. "I am a changed man, I confess, and I have her to thank for such a transformation."

"I am not quite certain how to respond to such news." Lord Hogarth closed his eyes for a few seconds, then opened them again and stared at Patrick with such intent that Patrick wondered if his friend was attempting to make certain that he had not gone mad. "You must tell me her name." Taking a small step closer and appearing to recover himself a little more, Lord Hogarth dropped his head. "Is it someone present here this evening?"

"As I have said, pray do not ask me." Patrick grinned

then turned to bow to one particular young lady who had come to join them. "In fact, I must beg you to excuse me. I am sure, Miss Howick, that Lord Hogarth would be *glad* to dance with you..."

Leaving the surprised young lady and the even more astonished Lord Hogarth behind, Patrick turned on his heel and made his way through the crowd. He wanted nothing more than to be in Lady Albina's company again, to confess the truth, and to tell her what he now found himself hoping for between them.

Hurrying up through the house, he left the noise of the Ball behind him. His heart was filled with all manner of happiness, his mind settled, and his decision made. If she accepted him, Patrick did not doubt that there would be difficulties in their future, but that would be nothing compared with what joy they would share. Lady Albina was, to Patrick's mind, the most incredible lady. She had risked her reputation to escape from Lord Kingston and had found an entirely new situation for herself. Patrick thought well of her determination and her courage. There was, he was certain, no other young lady like her, and now that he considered that, it came as no surprise that he had fallen in love with her.

A smile on his lips, Patrick began to climb the staircase towards the schoolroom and nursery. Lady Albina would have already settled Henry, but he prayed that she would still be awake. Perhaps she would be in the schoolroom, preparing Henry's lessons. Just the thought of putting his arms around her and holding her close sent such a jolt of excited anticipation into Patrick's heart that he began to take the stairs two at a time.

Recalling that he ought to be a little quieter given that Henry would be asleep, Patrick kept his steps slow as he made his way first to the schoolroom. He did not knock but stepped inside, seeing the flickering candle sitting on the desk. There were some papers open beside it but no sign of Lady Albina.

Patrick frowned, stepped back, and closed the door again. Mayhap she had gone to settle Henry once more or had gone to her bedchamber for something. It would not be wise to leave a candle burning in the schoolroom for the remainder of the evening and Patrick did not think that Lady Albina would be so foolish. Turning his head this way and that, he chose then to go next to the nursery, in case she should be waiting there.

A sudden noise made him jump. Looking over his shoulder and wishing that there were more than just one or two candles lit in the hallway for him to see by, Patrick's heart began to hammer furiously as the sound came again. It was as if something were being pushed aside or moved out of the way, for the sound scraped and scuffed and echoed down the walls. More than a little confused, Patrick looked about him but could see nothing.

"Miss Trean?"

He did not want to call out for Lady Albina for fear that someone else was present and would overhear him. The sound stopped, however, and Patrick was left standing quietly in the hallway, the only sound now the roaring of blood in his ears.

Frowning, he walked directly to the nursery, ignoring the creaks of the floorboards beneath his feet. Fumbling his way to the fireplace, he found a candle and quickly lit it, holding it aloft. *Clearly, Lady Albina is not here, given that the nursery is in darkness.* Grimacing, Patrick did not return to the door immediately but walked all around the room, although quite what he was searching for, he did not know.

Something is wrong.

He was not sure what it was that made him think so, but his instincts told him that all was not well. Walking out of the nursery, he hurried to Henry's room and pushed open the door.

Relief swamped him as his eyes adjusted to the gloom and he saw the dark-haired boy sound asleep in his bed. Hearing the boy's steady, rhythmic breathing, Patrick crept inside and, holding his candle aloft, looked all around.

Lady Albina was not here. Which meant that the only other place she might be would be her bedchamber. Mayhap, after she had spent some time in the schoolroom, she had been required to fetch something from there before returning.

The sense of foreboding did not leave him, however. Patrick closed Henry's door carefully and then returned to the schoolroom. The candle still burned, but Lady Albina was still notably absent. And when he went to her bedchamber and knocked, there was no answer.

"Lady Albina?" Speaking quietly, Patrick knocked on the door again. "I do not wish to disturb you but there is a matter of importance which I should very much like to speak to you about, just as soon as possible. If you are presentable, might you be able to attend me in the schoolroom?"

Silence answered his question. The third time he knocked, the sound seemed to laugh at him, as though he were being quite ridiculous.

Mayhap she is asleep.

Patrick shook his head to himself. If she were asleep, then why was there a candle burning in the schoolroom? Lady Albina would not have been as foolish as to leave it there, he was sure. He had to be sure. He had to know for certain that she either was or was not in her bedchamber.

Rapping smartly on the door again, Patrick cleared his throat.

"You will forgive me, I hope?"

Pushing the door open, he held the candle a little higher as he stepped inside.

There was no squeal of protest, no demand that he leave the room at once. Instead, the silence which lingered there seemed to mock him, laughing at his hope that Lady Albina would be present. His stomach twisted, his lips bunching together as his mind began to whirr with ideas. Just where was Lady Albina? He could not imagine that she had gone downstairs, not on the very same evening as the Ball, unless she had gone in search of something to eat? His concern grew steadily until it was a thick, dark cloud which hung over his head. Just where could Lady Albina be?

"A gentleman has taken her."

Patrick swung around, his heart screaming in shock and his whole body alive with a sudden, fierce tension.

"I have tried to stop him, but he is now attempting to steal your smallest carriage. We must hurry."

Holding his candle higher, Patrick took a slow, careful step forward. He recognized the voice, but his mind could not grasp the truth of it. As the light began to flicker across the gentleman's face, Patrick caught his breath, hardly able to take it in. A thousand questions burned through his mind at once, but he could not utter a single one of them. His eyes flared and his breath hitched, astonished beyond any comprehension.

His brother, James Dutton, was standing in the doorway of Lady Albina's bedchamber, as though he had never been lost at all.

"I know that you will have a great many questions, but now is not the time for me to answer them." His brother took a step forward and put his hand on Patrick's shoulder, as if to prove to him that he was *not* a ghost or apparition. "We must get to the stables. I attempted to stop him myself but had not the ability to prevent him from preparing and taking your carriage and so I returned here in the hope that I could convince someone to help."

Patrick nodded, trying to dispel the shock which currently held him captive.

"Lord Kingston has taken Lady Albina."

"I did not hear all of the conversation, but I believe Lord Kingston was greatly astonished over some matter or other." His brother tilted his head. "She is not 'Miss Trean', then?"

Wanting to ask how his brother knew that the lady had been using such a name, but lacking time, Patrick merely nodded.

"That would explain the loud exclamations, then." Turning in the doorway, Dutton beckoned towards Patrick. "Come. We must go at once."

Patrick forced himself to act, his limbs feeling wooden as he followed his brother. There was no simple explanation for his sudden reappearance, but that was not the pressing matter at hand. Patrick's steps grew quicker as fire began to burn through his veins. Lord Kingston had not taken his leave, as Patrick had assumed. Instead, he had returned in secret and had made his way directly to Lady Albina. The fellow did not like being refused what he so obviously wanted, for Patrick was in no doubt that Lord Kingston had intended to have his way with the governess, simply so that he would not return to London having been denied what it was he wanted. Patrick could not imagine the shock that the man would have felt upon seeing Lady Albina standing before him, nor the horror which would have swarmed through the lady.

I am coming to find you, Albina. His jaw tightened, his hands tightening into fists. *And this time, I will never let you go again.*

CHAPTER FOURTEEN

"Kingston."

Albina pressed one hand to her stomach as Lord Kingston's expression turned from glee to utter shock. She had turned towards him as he'd opened the door and there was no hiding the truth any longer. Fear tied itself in knots in her core as she stared back at him, not understanding either how or why he had returned to the manor house. Lord Addenbrook had thrown him from it but now, it seemed, he had come back.

And he had done so solely for her.

Albina shuddered but did not move. From the expression on Lord Kingston's face, it was clear that he had not had any prior knowledge of the truth of her identity. He had returned simply so that he might take what he wanted from her so that he would not be denied.

The filth in his character sickened her.

"Well, well." Lord Kingston slowly began to smile as he stepped into the room a little more. "I cannot quite believe what I am seeing, but it has all suddenly become very clear."

Chuckling, he reached out one hand, but Albina backed

away, stumbling slightly as she hit the edge of the bed. The room was small and there was nowhere else for her to go, nowhere else to turn. She had stepped out of the schoolroom for a few short moments, intending to find her shawl, but now was trapped by the presence of the gentleman she had hoped never to lay eyes on again.

"You have no right to be in here, Kingston." Her voice was a little tremulous, but Albina took in a deep breath, determined not to be moved. "I am under Lord Addenbrook's protection."

Lord Kingston chuckled.

"And does he know the truth? That you are *not* Miss Trean?"

Albina lifted her chin.

"He does." That took some of the bite from Lord Kingston's smile. "And you should leave before you are discovered." Albina flung the shawl around her shoulders and pinned him with her gaze. "I have duties I must fulfill."

The narrowing of Lord Kingston's eyes told Albina that he was not about to be so easily moved.

"You will return to London with me."

"I shall do no such thing." Her voice grew louder. "I have already made it quite clear that I have no intention of marrying you. I am quite resolute."

His hand shot out before she could say another word, grasping hard at her arm, and Albina could not prevent her yelp of pain.

"You shall do as you are told, *Miss Trean*," he snarled, his face now close to hers, vehemence in every word and every look. "Do you truly believe that I would leave you here, now that I know the truth? Your parents would never forgive me."

Albina tried to squirm out of his grasp, but it was no

good. Lord Kingston was a good deal stronger than she and his fingers were already leaving pain ripping across her skin.

"Do not flatter yourself that you have any sort of good in your character."

That earned her a slap which left her teeth rattling and her face burning.

"I would not leave you here no matter how hard you begged." His breath was hot across her face, her arm wrenched as he pulled her back hard against him. "Whether or not Lord Addenbrook knows of your true identity, you cannot stay here. You are meant to be my bride and I *will* have you. You *and* your dowry."

Albina wanted to state that he would never be her husband, but the pain in her cheek was beginning to spread up to her head and around into her neck and she could barely put two words together. It took her a few moments to realize that he was pulling her out of her bedchamber and through the hallway. She stumbled and almost fell on the stairs, but he hauled her alongside him and forced her to keep step with him. His hand was still on her arm, his other hand wrapped about her waist in an attempt to keep her beside him.

He took her out of the house through the servants' back entrance, and across the gravel to the stables and the carriage house. Albina wanted to cry out but could not seem to form a single sound. Shock and pain kept her from speaking, and it was not until she was flung, hard, against something that she finally let out a cry of pain.

"Stay there, or it will be all the worse for you."

Lord Kingston had flung her against the door of one of Lord Addenbrook's carriages. None of the stable hands appeared to be present – they would be taking care of the guests' horses, she realized. Pushing herself up to standing,

Albina leaned back against the carriage and drew in a deep breath. The stable was dimly lit by various lanterns and the shadows which roved around her threatened to take her very breath from her. Fear was tying itself to her heart, refusing to let her free, and Albina dropped her head. Her back, shoulders, and chest were tight with pain from where Lord Kingston had thrown her, her arm hot from where his fingers had dug into her skin. She could try to run, but Lord Kingston was faster and stronger than she, and Albina was afraid of what he would do if he caught her.

Something, a small movement, caught her gaze. Albina blinked, hard, trying to make the figure out clearly. A man was peering around the side of the carriage house door, staring at her, his face illuminated by a small, flickering lantern hung on the wall near him. Albina did not recognize him, but she lifted one hand out towards him in the hope that he would help her – but upon seeing her do so, the man disappeared back into the shadows, leaving her hand to fall to her side in hopelessness.

You cannot just stand here and do as Lord Kingston demands, she told herself, trying to garner a little courage. *If you flee into the darkness, then surely he will not know where you have gone? You know the grounds better than he does. It will not be too difficult to find a place to hide.*

"Sit down." Lord Kingston stormed towards her, anger evident in the lift of his shoulders and the fierceness of his steps. "I did not tell you to stand." Again, he thrust her back and Albina's head smacked hard against the carriage door. Sinking down onto the cold stone floor, she did as she was asked without hesitation, setting her teeth against the pain in her head. Lord Kingston glared at her and then turned back to his preparations. She could hear him muttering his frustrations, obviously irritated that he was now having to ready the carriage alone. She wondered, then, if he had ever harnessed horses to a carriage for himself, before. The thought made her want to laugh – for if he did not know how, did not know the horses, then his plans would be a failure from the start.

Shuddering, Albina closed her eyes tightly, realizing that, when he had thought her just the governess, he had never had any intention of taking her with him. He had only wanted to make sure that he had taken *from* her what he had wanted and then would have happily returned home, leaving her behind.

I can never marry him.

Despite the pain in her head and body, Albina lifted her chin and tried to think of a plan. Lord Kingston was still too close for her to make any attempt at running away, but the moment he stepped out of sight - which he would have to do, to fetch the single horse that this small carriage required - she would push herself to her feet and hurry away. Yes, he might catch her and yes, he might succeed in forcing her into the carriage, but she would not simply sit here and become a biddable, subservient creature who did precisely as was asked. She knew herself better than that.

There is the small thicket to the left of the stables, she reminded herself. *Or I could try to find the stable hands and beg for their help. Lord Kingston would not dare attempt to force me then.*

"Whatever it is you are thinking, rid yourself of it now." Lord Kingston's hand clamped down on her shoulder. "You will not succeed this time, Albina. You are to be my wife."

She lifted her face to his.

"Never." Her eyes were set, her voice cool. "I will do all that I can to escape you, whether it be this day, tomorrow, or even as your wife. I will do all that I can to run from you, to unbind myself from you. You will have no success here, Kingston. I will never be the obedient wife you so hope for."

For a moment, she thought he would strike her but, even though his eyes narrowed, and his lip curled into a sneer, he did not do so.

"I am sure I will be able to remove that disobedient spirit from you one way or the other," he murmured, sending a shudder down Albina's spine. "You will have no opportunity for escape once we are wed. And I intend to obtain a special license so that it may take place just as soon as is possible. The debts that I owe will not pay themselves, after all, and your dowry is the finest one in all of London, I think!"

I knew he wanted my dowry. His words and dark looks sent another tremor of fear through her, but Albina hid it from her expression as best she could. Holding his gaze steadily, she waited until he dropped his eyes and turned away before letting out a long, slow breath which rattled out of her lungs.

I have to escape him.

Taking steadying breaths, Albina gathered up her skirts carefully and prepared herself for the moment when she could surge to her feet and run. Her eyes dragged towards Lord Kingston time and again before, finally, he rounded the end of the carriage and stepped out of her sight, going towards the door into the stables proper.

The rustle of her skirts seemed like thunder in her ears, but Albina was on her feet in a second. She did not even attempt to walk quietly and stealthily but ran, full pelt, out of the door and into the cool evening air. It did not take but a moment for Lord Kingston to realize that she was gone – perhaps he had heard her footsteps - and she heard him shout, heard his feet pounding just behind her.

The darkness opened up towards her and Albina ran headlong into it, not certain where she was going or in what direction she was meant to be going. The moon was gone behind a cloud and the darkness was thick. With the cloak of fear still tight around her and her mind screaming at her to run, Albina searched desperately for somewhere to go, somewhere to hide.

"Albina!"

Lord Kingston was no longer trying to be at all discreet. His voice bellowed out across the grounds and Albina's heart slammed furiously against her chest in a panic.

She turned her head this way and that, finally realizing that the lights from the manor house were behind her. Turning, she stopped dead for a few moments, wondering if she dared go back the way she had come for fear that Lord Kingston would discover her.

A lantern light caught her attention. It was bobbing slowly towards her, perhaps clutched in someone's hand. Albina's throat locked and she closed her eyes. Was that Lord Kingston? Had he grasped a lantern from the stable wall and come in search of her?

"Albina?"

The voice this time was not that of Lord Kingston. Albina's eyes flared, hardly able to trust what she had heard.

"Albina! Where are you?"

Addenbrook.

She moved quickly, stumbling as her feet caught on a root. She dared not call out for fear that Lord Kingston would reach her first.

"Albina!"

Her hands reached out towards the lantern light, her eyes rounding, her heart filling with relief – until a hand reached out and grabbed her.

"We shall avoid Lord Addenbrook, I think." Lord Kingston hissed in her ear, pulling her back from the light, tugging her away. "You shall not escape me this time."

Albina whirled around, ignoring the way his fingers tore into the soft skin by her neck. As hard as she could, she thrust her foot down, managing to land her heel on Lord Kingston's foot, although he only grunted. The elbow that she thrust out, however, managed to catch him off-guard and he let out a yelp of surprise. Albina, tearing herself away, began to run heedlessly - in any direction, so long as it was away from Lord Kingston.

She collided with something solid.

A scream ripped from her throat as she fought to escape from the tight arms which wrapped themselves around her waist. Kicking and pushing back, it took her a moment to realize that the voice which spoke to her was not that of Lord Kingston.

"Albina. Albina! It is I, do not struggle so. You are safe. You are quite safe."

A sob tore from her throat.

"Addenbrook." All the fight and fear went from her in an instant as she sagged against him, her arms about his neck and her head falling gently onto his shoulder. He held her, one arm about her waist as the other rubbed her back, and he murmured soft words into her ear. Her head lifted suddenly. "Lord Kingston! He is–"

"My brother has gone in search of him." Albina stilled, unable to comprehend what he had said. "I do not quite understand it but yes, my brother has reappeared, and all is well with him. When we heard your scream, we both began to run towards the sound – but then you fell into my arms, and I have no doubt that Dutton will catch Lord Kingston." His lips caught her cheek and Albina sank back into his arms, weary beyond explanation. "Come, let me take you back to the house. There is much you must tell me."

Albina did not lift her head.

"Is Henry quite all right?"

"He is quite well," Lord Addenbrook promised. "Sound asleep when I left him, in fact. You need not worry one iota, my dear Albina. He is safe." She cried then, letting the tears roll down her cheeks and onto his shirt. "*You* are safe, my dear Albina." Lord Addenbrook's lips brushed lightly against her cheek. "You need never worry about Lord Kingston again."

CHAPTER FIFTEEN

It took some time for Lady Albina to recover, but Patrick did not want to begin any sort of discussion or explanation before she was ready. Lord Kingston had been hauled back indoors by Dutton and a couple of stable hands who had overheard the commotion, and he was presently locked in one of the unused servants' rooms with nothing but a bed and a chair to keep him company. Patrick did not care about the gentleman's lack of comfort. After what he had done to Lady Albina, part of him wanted to keep the fellow locked up for the rest of his days, such was his fury.

"Albina."

He moved towards her the moment she opened the door. Her face was pale, but she smiled at him, her eyes soft and her hands reaching out for his. Grasping them, Patrick resisted the urge to pull her into his arms, not when his brother was present. It was enough just to have her in his company again.

"Thank you, Addenbrook."

He shook his head.

"There is no need to thank me. You were attempting to escape from Lord Kingston before we even arrived!"

"I was afraid he would catch me."

The smile fled from her lips, she shivered, and Patrick could not help but tug her close.

"He did not," he murmured, as his brother turned his back on them, looking out of the window into the dark night as if there was something incredibly interesting for him to see. "Now you are free of him for good."

She looked up at him, a question in her eyes – but it was not one that he could answer at present.

"Do forgive me."

The door opened and Patrick stepped back from Lady Albina, although he did keep her hand in his.

"Hogarth? Whatever is the matter?"

The Ball was still in full swing and Patrick was rather surprised to see his friend.

Lord Hogarth shook his head, giving Lady Albina a quick look but otherwise ignoring her.

"It was just when you stated that you intended to go to London as soon as you could to speak to your brother's man of business. I had thought to offer you company." Shrugging, he spread his hands. "Since I am departing tomorrow also, I have now decided to make my way to London also. We might drive together."

Patrick frowned, completely confused as to why Lord Hogarth wished to speak of such a thing *now*.

"I thank you, but no." Seeing his friend's lips twist hard and him look away sharply, Patrick tilted his head. "Is there some reason that you require my company?"

Lord Hogarth shrugged.

"No, nothing in particular."

"Are you quite sure?"

Even Patrick, who had known that his brother was present in the room, started in surprise, but it was Lord Hogarth who began to stutter.

"I think you should tell my brother the truth, Hogarth." Dutton began to come forward, his hands clasped behind his back. "Why do you not tell him about the threats that you placed upon my head?"

Shock pinned Patrick to the floor.

"Threats?" he repeated, as his brother nodded firmly, although still looking at Lord Hogarth. "Why did you not tell me any of this?"

Dutton stopped then gestured to Lord Hogarth.

"I believe this man's final words to me were, 'if you tell anyone of this matter, then your son will suffer severe consequences'." He lifted one eyebrow. "I knew from experience that you would do as you had threatened, Hogarth, and I could not take the risk of remaining alone at my estate with Henry to care for." His eyes darted towards Patrick's. "And thus, we came here. I told Henry that I would be absent for a short while but that I would return – and then I left my carriage and sent it on to you, brother."

Patrick's chest was tight and his every breath difficult. Struggling to comprehend what his brother was saying, he turned his attention to Lord Hogarth, expecting him either to deny everything or to tell him that it was not *exactly* as Dutton now explained it.

What he saw told Patrick that he was mistaken in that expectation. Lord Hogarth's lip was curling, his arms were tight, and his hands clenched. The way his shoulders lifted and his jaw jutted made Patrick step forward, suddenly afraid that Lord Hogarth would attack Dutton.

"You threatened my nephew?"

Lord Hogarth spat an exclamation at him but did not remove his eyes from Dutton.

"Ha! You speak as though I had no cause to say such things!"

"And what cause was that?" Patrick asked, aware of the tremor of anger in his voice. "If it was that my brother owed you some debt or other, you could have come to ask me – or my brother could."

Dutton spread his hands.

"I should have done so," he agreed, quietly. "But I did not. You have always prided yourself on being the wealthiest, most admired fellow, whereas I have struggled with my own foolishness and lost a good deal of what I once had." He threw Patrick a glance but did not hold his gaze. "I have asked you for assistance before and I could not bring myself to do it again."

Shame piled itself onto Patrick's shoulders.

"You should always be able to come to me for assistance, Dutton. I am ashamed of myself for putting appearance before everything else." Lady Albina's hand pressed his for just a moment and gratitude swelled Patrick's heart. Had she not arrived, then this situation might have been a good deal worse. He turned to his friend. "And you were all too aware of my brother's penchant for gambling. And yet you were eager to encourage him into such games?"

Scowling, Lord Hogarth's brows lowered over his eyes.

"It is not my fault if your brother is inclined towards such things."

"But it *is* your doing if you encourage him specifically in the hope of gaining some of his fortune," Patrick retorted, neither hearing nor seeing any denial of such a thing on his friend's face. Anger swirled with frustration that his brother had not come to him to beg for his help, whilst his anger also grew steadily towards Lord Hogarth. "I trusted you. I spoke to you about my brother without having even a thought that you would use such information for your own advantage!"

Lord Hogarth said nothing, and Patrick's anger burned all the hotter.

"I have no intention of gambling again," Dutton said heavily. "I owed Lord Hogarth a significant sum, Addenbrook. I paid him what I could and promised that the rest would come in time, but he would not wait." Throwing up one hand towards Lord Hogarth, he closed his eyes. "When he threatened to injure Henry, I knew that I had to do something to keep my son safe and so, I made arrangements to come here. My initial thought was to simply live a quiet existence elsewhere until the next quarter's income was given me so that I might then repay Lord Hogarth but, upon realizing that he was here for that first house party, I had no other choice but to hide myself in your house."

Lady Albina suddenly caught her breath, her eyes wide as she stared at Dutton.

"Yes, I remained close to Henry," Dutton continued, as if he knew the reason for her shock. "My brother does not know it, but there is a secret panel in the hallway next to Henry's bedchamber."

Patrick began to stutter, his eyes wide, even as Lady Albina spoke.

"Henry told me that you often bade him goodnight, but I thought it was only his childlike hope of your return!" Lady Albina's voice was thready, her face a little pale. "But you came out each evening to speak with him, did you not?"

Dutton smiled.

"I did." Turning to Patrick, he shrugged one shoulder. "You do not know of such things because you were never one to explore this house, not even when we were children,"

Dutton told him, a half-smile on his lips. "I used to hide from our governess for hours in that small space. Although it was a little more cramped now that I am no longer a child!"

This was almost too much to take in. Patrick blew out a long breath and raked both hands through his hair, suddenly feeling the need for a sip of brandy.

"Good gracious. When we were children, I often wondered where you had gone to."

"And now you know." Dutton spread his hands. "I used it to escape from Lord Hogarth's threats and to make certain that Henry was kept safe until I could understand what I needed to do next."

Lady Albina's hand covered her mouth as she gasped. All eyes turned to her as her hand slipped back to her side although her eyes were fixed on Lord Hogarth.

"And the messenger from London... that was your doing."

It took Patrick a moment to realize that he had spoken to Lord Hogarth about writing to Dutton's man of business – it seemed that, therefore, the attack on the messenger could be laid at his door.

"You did all you could to make certain that I would never find out the truth," he said slowly, as Lord Hogarth lifted his chin. "What did you do? Did you have a man at the inn, just waiting to...." Seeing Lord Hogarth's jaw tighten, Patrick realized he had hit upon the truth. "You are naught but a scoundrel, Hogarth. I am ashamed that I ever permitted myself to call you a friend."

Lady Albina moved to stand closer to Patrick, her nearness a gentle comfort.

"Do you have any explanation for such actions, Lord Hogarth?"

Lord Hogarth's lips tightened, and he turned his head away from her.

"I have no need to explain myself."

"You threatened my brother *and* my nephew." Patrick's voice rose and he took a step closer to the man he had once thought of as the very dearest of friends. "If you had really wanted that money, you could have spoken to me. You know that I have enough wealth to cover my brother's debts." Seeing the gleam in Lord Hogarth's eyes, Patrick's stomach dropped. "But you wanted the control, did you not? You wanted to be the one to hold sway over him, to be seen as powerful and intimidating."

Lord Hogarth rounded on him.

"It is not as though *you* can point the finger at me, Addenbrook. You are exactly the same as I!"

Patrick shook his head.

"That is not so. I confess that I have always sought to be admired, to be well thought of, and indeed, to make others look up to me, but I have *never* wanted to dominate or terrify others. I have no such cruelty and whilst that is of little merit given my other failures, I will not permit you to make us both so alike." Drawing closer, Patrick's arms grew tense, wanting to do nothing more than plant a facer onto Lord Hogarth's arrogant, smug expression. "You are no longer welcome in my house *or* in my company."

Lord Hogarth snorted.

"And your debts, Dutton?"

He looked past Patrick towards his brother, but Patrick grabbed Lord Hogarth's collar, forcing the man to look back at him, and for the first time, Patrick saw the flicker of fear in his eyes.

"*I* will pay whatever it is you require," he stated, his voice rough as he fought to keep his temper. "And bear in mind, Hogarth, that since we have been friends for a good many years, there is a much that I know about you. Much that I could impart to the *ton*, should you decide that you wish to speak less than positively about my brother, my nephew, or myself to anyone in society." The flicker in Lord Hogarth's eyes increased and he gave a small, jerky nod. Patrick dropped his hand, satisfied. It was no great punishment, but it was a promise of consequences should Lord Hogarth decide to speak ill of either himself or Dutton. Confident that Lord Hogarth would never dream of doing any such thing now, Patrick took a step back. "You are to leave my house within the hour. Dutton, ring the bell so that I might inform my staff to help Lord Hogarth return home."

Lord Hogarth did not say a word, but stood exactly where he was, unmoving. Patrick's frame grew tight with tension, but Lady Albina's hand settled on his and pushed some of that from him. Taking in a deep breath, he waited until Lord Hogarth finally decided to leave the room, refusing to say another word - although, had it not been for Lady Albina's restraining hand, he might well have physically forced Lord Hogarth out of his house.

The door closed behind Lord Hogarth, only to open again as the enquiring butler came to see what it was that Patrick wanted. Speaking in short, clipped tones, Patrick quickly informed him that Lord Hogarth was to depart the house and that the butler was to make certain it was done as soon as possible. He knew that it was a good deal to ask of his staff during the grand Ball but his only concern at present was for Lord Hogarth's presence to be gone from his house entirely – never to return.

"And now I must apologize to you, Lady Albina." Dutton cleared his throat and then bowed low towards her, as her hand squeezed Patrick's gently. "I did not mean to startle you the night that you fell. I heard someone coming and darted into the schoolroom. I did not manage to douse my light in time and was certain that you had seen me. So, out of fear of being discovered, I ran from the room and prayed that the shadows would hide my face."

Patrick closed his eyes, recalling just how dazed Lady Albina had been.

"That was you."

"It was, and I am heartily sorry. I did not mean to injure you, Lady Albina."

"That is quite all right." The softness in her voice was a balm to Patrick's tormented soul. "I understand that you were only doing what you thought was best to keep Henry safe. I cannot hold anything against you."

Dutton bowed.

"You are most generous, Lady Albina." He lifted his head and then turned to Patrick. "I am sorry, brother."

The ache that formed in Patrick's heart began to move towards his throat and he cleared it gruffly, attempting to push it away.

"You need not apologize, Dutton. I only wish that you had been able to tell me of your troubles long before any of this took place." A heavy sigh broke from his lips as he passed one hand over his eyes. "But I look at my character and how both yourself and Lord Hogarth viewed me, and I can understand why you did not."

Lady Albina pressed his hand and moved to stand a little closer to him.

"You must not blame yourself for this matter. This was all Lord Hogarth's doing."

"Indeed," his brother agreed, his hand on Patrick's shoulder. "I am grateful indeed for the care you have shown to Henry. I knew that I could trust you with the most precious of my possessions and that speaks very highly of you, brother."

Patrick released Lady Albina's hand and reached out to shake his brother's hand instead.

"It is thanks to Lady Albina that I have come to realize just how precious a child he is," he told him. "She is the one who has shown me what is important and what is not. I swear to you that I shall never return to being that arrogant, prideful gentleman who puts appearances above all else."

Dutton smiled and shook Patrick's hand firmly.

"And for my part, I shall never again permit myself to gamble." The smile on his face dimmed. "I have seen the danger it can bring, and I will never again sit at the card table, not for the rest of my days."

"But I will still clear your debts, such as they are." Patrick was unequivocal in his decision. "You will have nothing to weigh on your mind save for your estate and your son."

Dutton swallowed hard but said nothing, only managing a small nod. Patrick smiled and released his brother's hand. There was more gratitude in his silence than Patrick could ever hear from Dutton's lips – but for himself, he did not need any such thing. All he wanted was for Dutton and Henry to return to their lives without fear.

"You will want to see Henry, of course." Lady Albina smiled gently at Dutton, who nodded again. "He will be asleep but –"

"That will not matter." Dutton's voice was brittle but his smile broad. "I will stay with him until he wakens and then I will tell him that he will never be apart from me again." Inclining his head, he quickly turned and left the room, his steps hasty as if he could not wait a single moment longer to be reunited with his son. Patrick's chest rose and fell as he took in one deep sigh, closing his eyes as the door shut behind his brother.

There was a peace in him now that he had not felt in a long time. His brother was returned. His nephew was safe and he himself was no longer pushed and pulled by the urgent desire to remain in as prominent a position as he could amongst society. The need to prove himself to be the wealthiest amongst his acquaintances was quite gone and, instead, what he had before him was the promise of a greater and more fulfilling happiness than he had ever imagined.

"Albina."

Turning to her, he took both her hands in his and shook his head to himself at the beauty who stood before him.

"This has been a very great shock, I am sure." Her smile was gentle, but he could see the weariness in her eyes. "Your brother has returned safely, however, and that must be an enormous relief."

"More than you could know," he replied, moving a little closer and intending to declare himself right then and there – just as a tap came to the door.

Lady Albina's eyes flared, and she stepped back, dropping her hands to her sides. A little nonplussed, it took Patrick a moment to recall that his household still considered her the governess and would not think well of her standing so close to him should they see it. Barking an order, he waited impatiently for the door to open, wanting to do nothing more than return to Lady Albina.

"My Lord, I beg your forgiveness, but the guests are in an uproar!"

The footman's eyes were a little wide as he spread his hands.

"We do not know what is to be done."

"An uproar?"

"They have been waiting for your return and now believe that something most untoward has occurred as one of the guests saw you step outside."

"I think you must return to your guests, my Lord." Lady Albina draped her persona of Miss Trean, the governess, back around her shoulders as she bobbed a curtsey. "Mayhap we might speak again tomorrow?"

The gentle twinkle in her eye made Patrick grimace.

"You cannot return to your bedchamber, Albina," he murmured so that the footman would not hear him. "You are the daughter of an Earl and –"

"I can be Miss Trean for one more night," she assured him. "Besides, I am very weary and will, no doubt, sleep very well indeed, regardless." The smile warmed his heart, but it was with great reluctance that he allowed her to depart. "Good evening, Lord Addenbrook."

With a heavy sigh, Patrick waved her away with one hand.

"Good evening, Miss Trean," he muttered, before begrudgingly turning his attention back to the footman and to his duties as host.

Tomorrow would be a new beginning for them all, and Patrick had every intention of making certain that Lady Albina was never separated from him again.

EPILOGUE

"My Lord?"
Albina peeked into the drawing-room but found it empty save for Lord Addenbrook. At the sight of her, he let out a small exclamation and practically threw himself out of his chair as he hurried towards her.

"You need not refer to me in such terms any longer."

She smiled as he caught her hands.

"But you might have been with the butler, and I did want to be careful."

"There is no need for caution any longer," he told her, sending a jolt of surprise from her head to her toes. "Henry is departing with my brother by the week's end, and I shall then be free to do as I please – and I have every intention of spending my next few days thereafter in one particular place with only one particular person for company."

Albina pressed her lips together, her heart quickening.

"Is that so?"

She had no fear that he would send her from his house, not any longer. Since the revelations of the previous evening, Albina had sensed a change within him, as though he had been offered a glimpse of something truly wonderful and had wanted to grasp at it with both hands.

"Albina, you cannot return home."

She shook her head.

"No, I cannot."

"And I cannot have you apart from me." His hands were warm on hers. "You fill my life with beauty, joy, and hope. You have shown me what is truly important. I am ashamed of what I used to consider to be important to me, for I now realize that those things have no merit whatsoever." Moving a little closer to her, his hand lifted to her cheek, his fingers brushing gently across her skin and sending a shiver of delight down her spine. "When I first found myself eager for your company, I was frustrated with myself for thinking such things of a governess. But when I learned the truth, I was swamped with such relief that I could hardly contain it." His hand skimmed down her neck, her shoulder, and her arm before catching her fingers again. "And in speaking to Lord Hogarth last evening, I realized just how foolish I was to even be considering what I might do next. There is only one thing I want, only one thing that I desire – and that is to be with you, Lady Albina."

Her heart soared.

"You speak of my own heart's desire also, Lord Addenbrook."

He smiled into her eyes.

"Then if I suggest that we take a short trip together to Scotland if we were perhaps to find a blacksmith and an anvil?" Unable to hold herself back, Albina flung her arms about his neck and laughed with joy. Lord Addenbrook's arms went about her, and she felt the soft rumble of his chest as he laughed with her. "Then you will marry me?" he asked, whispering those words into her ear. "You will become my wife?"

Albina pulled back a little and looked deeply into his eyes.

"I could not wish to ever be parted from you, Addenbrook," she answered, softly. "When I first arrived, I thought you arrogant and selfish. But I have seen you change. I have learned of the hurt and the struggle that you faced in the disappearance of your brother. I have seen you change your approach towards Henry and he, in turn, has warmed to you." Her hands pulled back from his neck, framing his face. "You protected me on more than one occasion and saved me from Lord Kingston's intentions. And now you are throwing aside what once held such importance for you to secure your future with me!" Seeing the tenderness in his expression, she smiled softly up at him. "Your heart is good and kind, and I cannot help but love you."

His lips descended to hers and Albina reached up on tiptoes to meet him. His lips were soft and warm, his hands tight about her waist as she leaned into him, her arms around his neck once more. She kissed him without hesitation, trusting him with both her present and her future. Joy like she'd never known seemed to sweep her away and, when she opened her eyes, stars sparkled in her vision.

"I love you, Albina."

Lord Addenbrook cupped her chin, his eyes searching her face as if desperate for her to believe him.

"I did not even think I was capable of such an emotion, but it is like a torrent pouring out from my heart. I love you. I love you desperately."

"Then make me your bride," she whispered, leaning against his strong frame, her fingers brushing through the hair at the back of his neck. "For my only wish is to be your wife."

He smiled, his eyes gleaming and, in the next moment, Albina found herself caught up in his arms.

"Then I shall have the carriage prepared immediately," he growled playfully, making her laugh. "And you shall have your dearest wish, Lady Albina, and I shall have mine." His head turned a little more and he caught her lips with his own again. "To be your dutiful, loving husband who will do nothing other than marvel at the day he found such a beautiful, tender lady such as you." He smiled into her eyes. "I love you, Albina."

Her hand brushed his cheek tenderly.

"I love you too."

I AM glad the Lady Albina found her true love and didn't have to return to her father's house! If you missed the first book in this series, here it is! More Than a Companion There is a preview just ahead. Or check out the list of all my books and find one you missed!

MY DEAR READER

Thank you for reading and supporting my books! I hope this story brought you some escape from the real world into the always captivating Regency world. A good story, especially one with a happy ending, just brightens your day and makes you feel good! If you enjoyed the book, would you leave a review on Amazon? Reviews are always appreciated.

Below is a complete list of all my books! Why not click and see if one of them can keep you entertained for a few hours?

The Duke's Daughters Series
The Duke's Daughters: A Sweet Regency Romance Boxset
A Rogue for a Lady
My Restless Earl
Rescued by an Earl
In the Arms of an Earl
The Reluctant Marquess (Prequel)

A Smithfield Market Regency Romance
The Smithfield Market Romances: A Sweet Regency Romance Boxset
The Rogue's Flower
Saved by the Scoundrel
Mending the Duke
The Baron's Malady

The Returned Lords of Grosvenor Square
The Returned Lords of Grosvenor Square: A Regency Romance Boxset
The Waiting Bride
The Long Return
The Duke's Saving Grace
A New Home for the Duke

The Spinsters Guild
The Spinsters Guild: A Sweet Regency Romance Boxset
A New Beginning
The Disgraced Bride
A Gentleman's Revenge
A Foolish Wager
A Lord Undone

Convenient Arrangements
Convenient Arrangements: A Regency Romance Collection
A Broken Betrothal
In Search of Love
Wed in Disgrace
Betrayal and Lies
A Past to Forget
Engaged to a Friend

Landon House
Mistaken for a Rake
A Selfish Heart
A Love Unbroken
A Christmas Match
A Most Suitable Bride
An Expectation of Love

Second Chance Regency Romance
Loving the Scarred Soldier
Second Chance for Love
A Family of her Own
A Spinster No More

Soldiers and Sweethearts
To Trust a Viscount
Whispers of the Heart
Dare to Love a Marquess
Healing the Earl
A Lady's Brave Heart

Ladies on their Own: Governesses and Companions
More Than a Companion
The Hidden Governess

Christmas Stories
Love and Christmas Wishes: Three Regency Romance Novellas
A Family for Christmas
Mistletoe Magic: A Regency Romance
Heart, Homes & Holidays: A Sweet Romance Anthology

Happy Reading!

All my love,

Rose

A SNEAK PEEK OF MORE THAN A COMPANION

PROLOGUE

"Did you hear me, Honora?"

Miss Honora Gregory lifted her head at once, knowing that her father did not refer to her as 'Honora' very often and that he only did so when he was either irritated or angry with her.

"I do apologize, father, I was lost in my book," Honora replied, choosing to be truthful with her father rather than make excuses, despite the ire she feared would now follow. "Forgive my lack of consideration."

This seemed to soften Lord Greene just a little, for his scowl faded and his lips were no longer taut.

"I shall only repeat myself the once," her father said firmly, although there was no longer that hint of frustration in his voice. "There is very little money, Nora. I cannot give you a Season."

All thought of her book fled from Honora's mind as her eyes fixed to her father's, her chest suddenly tight. She had known that her father was struggling financially, although she had never been permitted to be aware of the details. But not to have a Season was deeply upsetting, and Honora had to immediately fight back hot tears which sprang into her eyes. There had always been a little hope in her heart, had always been a flicker of expectation that, despite knowing her father's situation, he might still be able to take her to London."

"Your aunt, however, is eager to go to London," Lord Greene continued, as Honora pressed one hand to her stomach in an attempt to soothe the sudden rolling and writhing which had captured her. He waved a hand dismissively, his expression twisting. "I do not know the reasons for it, given that she is widowed and, despite that, happily settled, but it seems she is determined to have some time in London this summer. Therefore, whilst you are not to have a Season of your own – you will not be presented or the like – you will go with your aunt to London."

Honora swallowed against the tightness in her throat, her hands twisting at her gown as she fought against a myriad of emotions.

"I am to be her companion?" she said, her voice only just a whisper as her father nodded.

She had always been aware that Lady Langdon, her aunt, had only ever considered her own happiness and her own situation, but to invite your niece to London as your companion rather than chaperone her for a Season surely spoke of selfishness!

"It is not what you might have hoped for, I know," her father continued, sounding resigned as a small sigh escaped his lips, his shoulders slumping. Honora looked up at him, seeing him now a little grey and realizing the full extent of his weariness. Some of her upset faded as she took in her father's demeanor, knowing that his lack of financial security was not his doing. The estate lands had done poorly these last three years, what with drought one year and flooding the next. As such, money had been ploughed into the ground to restore it and yet it would not become profitable again for at least another year. She could not blame her father for that. And yet, her heart had struggled against such news, trying to be glad that she would be in London but broken-hearted to learn that her aunt wanted her as her companion and nothing more. "I will not join you, of course," Lord Greene continued, coming a little closer to Honora and tilting his head just a fraction, studying his daughter carefully and, perhaps, all too aware of her inner turmoil. "You can, of course, choose to refuse your aunt's invitation – but I can offer you nothing more than what is being given to you at present, Nora. This may be your only opportunity to be in London."

Honora blinked rapidly against the sudden flow of hot tears that threatened to pour from her eyes, should she permit them.

"It is very good of my aunt," she managed to say, trying to be both gracious and thankful whilst ignoring the other, more negative feelings which troubled her. "Of course, I shall go."

Lord Greene smiled sadly, then reached out and settled one hand on Honora's shoulder, bending down just a little as he did so.

"My dear girl, would that I could give you more. You already have enough to endure, with the loss of your mother when you were just a child yourself. And now you have a poor father who cannot provide for you as he ought."

"I understand, Father," Honora replied quickly, not wanting to have her father's soul laden with guilt. "Pray, do not concern yourself. I shall be contented enough with what Lady Langdon has offered me."

Her father closed his eyes and let out another long sigh, accompanied this time with a shake of his head.

"She may be willing to allow you a little freedom, my dear girl," he said, without even the faintest trace of hope in his voice. "My sister has always been inclined to think only of herself, but there may yet be a change in her character."

Honora was still trying to accept the news that she was to be a companion to her aunt and could not make even a murmur of agreement. She closed her eyes, seeing a vision of herself standing in a ballroom, surrounded by ladies and gentlemen of the *ton*. She could almost hear the music, could almost feel the warmth on her skin... and then realized that she would be sitting quietly at the back of the room, able only to watch, and not to engage with any of it. Pain etched itself across her heart and Honora let out a long, slow breath, allowing the news to sink into her very soul.

"Thank you, Father." Her voice was hoarse but her words heartfelt, knowing that her father was doing his very best for her in the circumstances. "I will be a good companion for my aunt."

"I am sure that you will be, my dear," he said, quietly. "And I will pray that, despite everything, you might find a match – even in the difficulties that face us."

The smile faded from Honora's lips as, with that, her father left the room. There was very little chance of such a thing happening, as she was to be a companion rather than a debutante. The realization that she would be an afterthought, a lady worth nothing more than a mere glance from the moment that she set foot in London, began to tear away at Honora's heart, making her brow furrow and her lips pull downwards. There could be no moments of sheer enjoyment for her, no time when she was not considering all that was required of her as her aunt's companion. She would have to make certain that her thoughts were always fixed on her responsibilities, that her intentions were settled on her aunt at all times. Yes, there would be gentlemen to smile at and, on the rare chance, mayhap even converse with, but her aunt would not often permit such a thing, she was sure. Lady Langdon had her own reasons for going to London for the Season, whatever they were, and Honora was certain she would take every moment for herself.

"I must be grateful," Honora murmured to herself, setting aside her book completely as she rose from her chair and meandered towards the window.

Looking out at the grounds below, she took in the gardens, the pond to her right and the rose garden to her left. There were so many things here that held such beauty and, with it, such fond memories that there was a part of her, Honora had to admit, which did not want to leave it, did not want to set foot in London where she might find herself in a new and lower situation. There was security here, a comfort which encouraged her to remain, which told her to hold fast to all that she knew – but Honora was all too aware that she could not. Her future was not here. When her father passed away, if she was not wed, then Honora knew that she would be left to continue on as a companion, just to make certain that she had a home and enough coin for her later years. That was not the future she wanted but, she considered, it might very well be all that she could gain. Tears began to swell in her eyes, and she dropped her head, squeezing her eyes closed and forcing the tears back. This was the only opportunity she would have to go to London and, whilst it was not what she had hoped for, Honora had to accept it for what it was and begin to prepare herself for leaving her father's house – possibly, she considered, for good. Clasping both hands together, Honora drew in a long breath and let it out slowly as her eyes closed and her shoulders dropped.

A new part of her life was beginning. A new and unexpected future was being offered to her, and Honora had no other choice but to grasp it with both hands.

CHAPTER ONE

*P*ushing all doubt aside, Robert walked into White's with the air of someone who expected not only to be noticed, but to be greeted and exclaimed over in the most exaggerated manner. His chin lifted as he snapped his fingers towards one of the waiting footmen, giving him his request for the finest of brandies in short, sharp words. Then, he continued to make his way inside, his hands swinging loosely by his sides, his shoulders pulled back and his chest a little puffed out.

"Goodness, is that you?"

Robert grinned, his expectations seeming to be met, as a gentleman to his left rose to his feet and came towards him, only for him to stop suddenly and shake his head.

"Forgive me, you are not Lord Johnstone," he said, holding up both hands, palms out, towards Robert. "I thought that you were he, for you have a very similar appearance."

Grimacing, Robert shrugged and said not a word, making his way past the gentleman and finding a slight heat rising into his face. To be mistaken for another was one thing, but to remain entirely unrecognized was quite another! His doubts attempted to come rushing back. Surely someone would remember him, would remember what he had done last Season?

"Lord Crampton, good evening."

Much to his relief, Robert heard his title being spoken and turned his head to the right, seeing a gentleman sitting in a high-backed chair, a glass of brandy in his hand and a small smile on his face as he looked up at Robert.

"Good evening, Lord Marchmont," Robert replied, glad indeed that someone, at least, had recognized him. "I am back in London, as you can see."

"I hope you find it a pleasant visit," came the reply, only for Lord Marchmont to turn away and continue speaking to another gentleman sitting opposite – a man whom Robert had neither seen, nor was acquainted with. There was no suggestion from Lord Marchmont about introducing Robert to him and, irritated, Robert turned sharply away. His head dropped, his shoulders rounded, and he did not even attempt to keep his frustration out of his expression. His jaw tightened, his eyes blazed and his hands balled into fists.

Had they all forgotten him so quickly?

Practically flinging himself into a large, overstuffed armchair in the corner of White's, Robert began to mutter darkly to himself, almost angry about how he had been treated. Last Season he had been the talk of London! Why should he be so easily forgotten now? Unpleasant memories rose, of being inconspicuous, and disregarded, when he had first inherited his title. He attempted to push them aside, but his upset grew steadily so that even the brandy he was given by the footman – who had spent some minutes trying to find Lord Crampton – tasted like ash in his mouth. Nothing took his upset away and Robert wrapped it around his shoulders like a blanket, huddling against it and keeping it close to him.

He had not expected this. He had hoped to be not only remembered but celebrated! When he stepped into a room, he thought that he should be noticed. He *wanted* his name to be murmured by others, for it to be spread around the room that he had arrived! Instead, he was left with an almost painful frustration that he had been so quickly forgotten by the *ton* who, only a few months ago, had been his adoring admirers.

"Another brandy might help remove that look from your face." Robert did not so much as blink, hearing the man's voice but barely acknowledging it. "You are upset, I can tell." The man rose and came to sit opposite Robert, who finally was forced to recognize him. "That is no way for a gentleman to appear upon his first few days in London!"

Robert's lip curled. He should not, he knew, express his frustration so openly, but he found that he could not help himself.

"Good evening, Lord Burnley," he muttered, finding the man's broad smile and bright eyes to be nothing more than an irritation. "Are *you* enjoying the London Season thus far?"

Lord Burnley chuckled, his eyes dancing - which added to Robert's irritation all the more. He wanted to turn his head away, to make it plain to Lord Burnley that he did not enjoy his company and wanted very much to be free of it, but his standing as a gentleman would not permit him to do so.

"I have only been here a sennight but yes, I have found

a great deal of enjoyment thus far," Lord Burnley told him. "But you should expect that, should you not? After all, a gentleman coming to London for the Season comes for good company, fine wine, excellent conversation and to be in the company of beautiful young ladies – one of whom might even catch his eye!"

This was, of course, suggestive of the fact that Lord Burnley might have had his head turned already by one of the young women making their come out, but Robert was in no mood to enter such a discussion. Instead, he merely sighed, picked up his glass again and held it out to the nearby footman, who came over to them at once.

"Another," he grunted, as the man took his glass from him. "And for Lord Burnley here."

Lord Burnley chuckled again, the sound grating on Robert's skin.

"I am quite contented with what I have at present, although I thank you for your consideration," he replied, making Robert's brow lift in surprise. What sort of gentleman turned down the opportunity to drink fine brandy? Half wishing that Lord Burnley would take his leave so that he might sit here in silence and roll around in his frustration, Robert settled back in his chair, his arms crossed over his chest and his gaze turned away from Lord Burnley in the vain hope that this would encourage the man to take his leave. He realized that he was behaving churlishly, yet somehow, he could not prevent it – he had hoped so much, and so far, nothing was as he had expected. "So, you are returned to London," Lord Burnley said, making Robert roll his eyes at the ridiculous observation which, for whatever reason, Lord Burnley either did not notice or chose to ignore. "Do you have any particular intentions for this Season?"

Sending a lazy glance towards Lord Burnley, Robert shrugged.

"If you mean to ask whether or not I intend to pursue one particular young lady with the thought of matrimony in mind, then I must tell you that you are mistaken to even *think* that I should care for such a thing," he stated, plainly. "I am here only to enjoy myself."

"I see."

Lord Burnley gave no comment in judgment of Robert's statement, but Robert felt it nonetheless, quite certain that Lord Burnley now thought less of him for being here solely for his own endeavors. He scowled. Lord Burnley might have decided that it was the right time for him to wed, but Robert had no intention of doing so whatsoever. Given his good character, given his standing and his title, there would be very few young ladies who would suit him, and Robert knew that it would take a significant effort not only to first identify such a young lady but also to then make certain that she would suit him completely. It was not something that he wanted to put his energy into at present. For the moment, Robert had every intention of simply dancing and conversing and mayhap even calling upon the young ladies of the *ton,* but that would be for his own enjoyment rather than out of any real consideration.

Besides which, he told himself, *given that the* ton *will, no doubt, remember all that you did last Season, there will be many young ladies seeking out your company which would make it all the more difficult to choose only one, should you have any inclination to do so!*

"And are you to attend Lord Newport's ball tomorrow evening?"

Being pulled from his thoughts was an irritating interruption and Robert let the long sigh fall from his lips without hesitation, sending it in Lord Burnley's direction who, much to Robert's frustration, did not even react to it.

"I am," Robert replied, grimacing. "Although I do hope that the other guests will not make too much of my arrival. I should not like to steal any attention away from Lord and Lady Newport."

Allowing himself a few moments of study, Robert looked back at Lord Burnley and waited to see if there was even a hint of awareness in his expression. Lord Burnley, however, merely shrugged one shoulder and turned his head away, making nothing at all of what Robert had told him. Gritting his teeth, Robert closed his eyes and tried to force out another long, calming breath. He did not need Lord Burnley to remember what he had done, nor to celebrate it. What was important was that the ladies of the *ton* recalled it, for then he would be more than certain to have their attention for the remainder of the Season – and that was precisely what Robert wanted. Their attention would elevate him in the eyes of the *ton*, would bring him into sharp relief against the other gentlemen who were enjoying the Season in London. He did not care what the gentlemen thought of him, he reminded himself, for their considerations were of no importance save for the fact that they might be able to invite him to various social occasions.

Robert's shoulders dropped and he opened his eyes. Coming to White's this evening had been a mistake. He ought to have made his way to some soiree or other, for he had many invitations already but, given that he had only arrived in London the day before, had thought it too early to make his entrance into society. That had been a mistake. The *ton* ought to know of his arrival just as soon as was possible, so that his name might begin to be whispered amongst them. He could not bear the idea that the pleasant notoriety he had experienced last Season might have faded already!

A small smile pulled at his lips as he considered this, his heart settling into a steady rhythm, free from frustration and upset now. Surely, it was not that he was not remembered by society, but rather that he had chosen the wrong place to make his entrance. The gentlemen of London would not make his return to society of any importance, given that they would be jealous and envious of his desirability in the eyes of the ladies of the *ton*, and therefore, he ought not to have expected such a thing from them! A quiet chuckle escaped his lips as Robert shook his head, passing one hand over his eyes for a moment. It had been a simple mistake and that mistake had brought him irritation and confusion – but that would soon be rectified, once he made his way into full London society.

"You appear to be in better spirits now, Lord Crampton."

Robert's brow lifted as he looked back at Lord Burnley, who was studying him with mild interest.

"I have just come to a realization," he answered, not wanting to go into a detailed explanation but at the same time, wanting to answer Lord Burnley's question. "I had hoped that I might have been greeted a little more warmly but, given my history, I realize now that I ought not to have expected it from a group of gentlemen."

Lord Burnley frowned.

"Your history?"

Robert's jaw tightened, wondering if it was truly that Lord Burnley did not know of what he spoke, or if he was saying such a thing simply to be a little irritating.

"You do not know?" he asked, his own brows drawing low over his eyes as he studied Lord Burnley's open expression. The man shook his head, his head tipping gently to one side in a questioning manner. "I am surprised. It was the talk of London!"

"Then I am certain you will be keen to inform me of it," Lord Burnley replied, his tone neither dull nor excited, making Robert's brow furrow all the more. "Was it something of significance?"

Robert gritted his teeth, finding it hard to believe that Lord Burnley, clearly present at last year's Season, did not know of what he spoke. For a moment, he thought he would not inform the fellow about it, given that he did not appear to be truly interested in what they spoke of, but then his pride won out and he began to explain.

"Are you acquainted with Lady Charlotte Fortescue?" he asked, seeing Lord Burnley shake his head. "She is the daughter of the Duke of Strathaven. Last Season, when I had only just stepped into the title of the Earl of Crampton, I discovered her being pulled away through Lord Kingsley's gardens by a most uncouth gentleman and, of course, in coming to her rescue, I struck the fellow a blow that had him knocked unconscious." His chin lifted slightly as he recalled that moment, remembering how Lady Charlotte had practically collapsed into his arms in the moments after he had struck the despicable Viscount Forthside and knocked him to the ground. Her father, the Duke of Strathaven, had been in search of his daughter and had found them both only a few minutes later, quickly followed by the Duchess of Strathaven. In fact, a small group of gentlemen and ladies had appeared in the gardens and had applauded him for his rescue – and news of it had quickly spread through London society. The Duke of Strathaven had been effusive in his appreciation and thankfulness for Robert's actions and Robert had reveled in it, finding that his newfound status within the *ton* was something to be enjoyed. He had assumed that it would continue into this Season and had told himself that, once he was at a ball or soiree with the ladies of the *ton*, his exaltation would continue. "The Duke and Duchess were, of course, very grateful," he finished, as Lord Burnley nodded slowly, although there was no exclamation of surprise on his lips nor a gasp of astonishment. "The gentlemen of London are likely a little envious of me, of course, but that is to be expected."

Much to his astonishment, Lord Burnley broke out into laughter at this statement, his eyes crinkling and his hand lifting his still-full glass towards Robert.

"Indeed, I am certain they are," he replied, his words filled with a sarcasm that could not be missed. "Good evening, Lord Crampton. I shall go now and tell the other gentlemen here in White's precisely who you are and what you have done. No doubt they shall come to speak to you at once, given your great and esteemed situation."

Robert set his jaw, his eyes a little narrowed as he watched Lord Burnley step away, all too aware of the man's cynicism. *It does not matter,* he told himself, firmly. *Lord Burnley, too, will be a little jealous of your success, and your standing in the* ton. *What else should you expect other than sarcasm and rebuttal?*

Rising to his feet, Robert set his shoulders and, with his head held high, made his way from White's, trying to ignore the niggle of doubt that entered his mind. Tomorrow, he told himself, he would find things much more improved. He would go to whatever occasion he wished and would find himself, of course, just as he had been last Season – practically revered by all those around him.

He could hardly wait.

CHECK out the rest of the story in the Kindle store. More Than a Companion

JOIN MY MAILING LIST

Sign up for my newsletter to stay up to date on new releases, contests, giveaways, freebies, and deals!

Free book with signup!

*Facebook Giveaways! Books and Amazon gift cards!
Join me on Facebook: https://www.facebook.com/rosepearsonauthor*

Website: www.RosePearsonAuthor.com

Follow me on Goodreads: Author Page

*You can also follow me on Bookbub!
Click on the picture below – see the Follow button?*

212 | JOIN MY MAILING LIST

Printed in Great Britain
by Amazon